Lila's Hamsa

Note: The *hamsa* is an amulet that in Judaism represents the hand of Miriam, the sister of Moses who placed him in the rushes. A stone in the center is thought to protect one from the evil eye. The name comes from the Hebrew for five, *hamesh*, the five fingers of the talisman. The *hamsa* is a common symbol in the Middle East. For the Muslims, it represents the hand of Fatima, one of the daughters of the Prophet Mohammad.

Lila's Hamsa

A Novel of Love and Deception

Arlene Kurtis

Rev. date: 09/12/2014

To order additional copies of this book, contact:
Xlibris LLC
1-888-795-4274
www.Xlibris.com
Orders@Xlibris.com
635357

Acknowledgments

I am eternally grateful to Martin Pomerance, my former editor, who made valuable suggestions and guided me during the writing of Lila's Hamsa. And to Joan Bier for reading and discussing the manuscript during its preparation.

I also wish to thank my many friends who shared experiences of their professional lives with me Thanks, too, to the folk at Xlibris for making it happen!

Chapter 1

On a cool October night in 1992, the road through the rural countryside was nearly deserted. The tractor-trailer driver was hauling his loaded rig at a smart clip, heading for home after a long day. He narrowed his eyes; something moved ahead. A doe disappeared into the woods. Then a buck leaped across his headlights! The driver swerved sharply to the left to avoid the animal, swinging the heavy trailer across the road as he braked. The driver looked behind him; no one was nearby. The green car must have exited at the rest stop a mile back. He could reverse, ease the rig around, turn safely, and maneuver his sixteen-wheeler back in lane. Breathing a sigh of relief, he drove on.

The green car had not exited; it had been in the teamster's blind spot. The rear of the trailer, like a batter swinging at the perfect pitch, lofted the rear of the green car over the guard rail onto a ledge. It teetered there for moments then rolled down to the precipice and fell into the gorge below. It smashed into a boulder and exploded in a rush of flames. The semi driver was around the bend by then; tuning his radio to get rid of static, he heard nothing.

Drivers gliding by, as dawn lightened the sky, could see a trail of smoke rising from below, but thought nothing of it. Only a day later, when the road crew rode along the shoulder, did a worker notice a car bumper and license plate lying on a tree stump. He stopped his truck and stepped over the guard rail. His gaze followed the wisp of smoke down into the gorge. He made out the crumpled frame of a burned-out car.

Police had to rappel into the gorge to examine the wreck. No one could survive such a crash, they agreed. Still, Anderson, the sergeant, instructed his men to comb the area for remains. There should be bones, teeth that survived the flames. Small bones were bagged, with sighs from the men on the scene. A child must have been aboard.

The lab reported the bones were from a raccoon. A wider area was searched. Nothing that could be tied to the victims was found.

Anderson was puzzled. What had they missed? He checked the local hospital with no result. At the rest stop, the day shift started at six o'clock, and the staff didn't remember any woman and child that early in the morning.

The license plate established that the car was owned by Lila Leif, who was born in 1965, so she'd be twenty-seven when the accident occurred. Her address was checked and the phone listed called.

"Lila left here about two years ago to get married," said the woman who rented apartments in her Victorian home to single teachers in the community. "She lives with her husband near the university. He's the genius there, they say."

"Were there any children?" Anderson asked.

"You'll have to call the university. I lost track of her after she came up in the world."

The reception desk at Rush University had no listing for Lila Leif, but the operator mentioned Lila Ostro, the wife of Professor Alton Ostro in the physics department. Anderson groaned. He hated the task of informing a family of disasters by phone; he took the long drive up to the university. Parking near the Science Triangle, he entered the physics building and asked the receptionist for the department head.

Dean Arthur Mayfield received him. "Yes, Lila's maiden name was Leif," he said, blanching when he heard the report. "My God," he said. "They were married two years ago with my blessing. I introduced them. She was a teacher in our demonstration pre-K school. I wanted Al to get out more, to have a social life. He's totally absorbed in his work. And they had a baby. Are you sure there are no survivors?"

"We can't rule it out, but I don't see how there could have been. The car was consumed by flames when it exploded down in the gorge. Another vehicle must have hit it to vault it over the guardrail. Any of a hundred vehicles could have been involved. We're looking into it, but it doesn't change things. I'm sorry," Anderson said. "How can we get in touch with the professor?"

"Down the hall, I'll go with you," Mayfield offered.

Back at headquarters, Bob Anderson, shook his head. "What a weird guy, this Ostro. He may be a genius, but he hardly showed any emotion. He asked no questions. Other than putting his head in hands for a minute, it seemed like he was listening to a story about total strangers."

"Any chance he might have been involved?" Captain DeAngelo asked.

"Checked that. He said he slept on the cot in his office—which he often does. The custodian confirmed. Ostro and his wife, it seems, went their separate ways. If she wasn't at home, he assumed she went to visit her brother in Pennsylvania. The car was headed in that direction. We got the name of the brother. He hadn't heard from her and didn't expect her."

Could the woman and child have survived the crash? "Not likely," Anderson told his captain. "She would have had to exit the car, go in the backdoor, unhitch the kid from the car seat, and get far enough away so that the car wouldn't hit her as it fell forward—all in moments? Impossible!"

The driver of the rig reported to his trucking company that he may have hit something as he swerved to avoid a deer. The side of his trailer had taken a dent when he jackknifed. The police asked to check the logs of drivers who might have been on the road at that time; the company admitted that one of their rigs had been in the area. The dent had been fixed, and the search for another vehicle was suspended. It was assumed that the semi was the cause of the crash.

Anderson's report on the search was given to Dr. Ostro. He had the option to sue. Meanwhile, the insurance company declined to pay the husband as the surviving spouse of the woman who held the title for the car, awaiting more evidence that Lila Ostro and Chloe Ostro had died. The husband accepted this. He was asked if he wanted a lawyer. He shook his head.

Later reviewing the file, Anderson questioned if the two passengers had, by some miracle, survived, wouldn't the mother have contacted someone by now? No one concerned had heard from them. Had they perished somewhere in those woods?

Chapter 2

Lila Ostro, in her little green car, was driving through the night to make Pittsburgh at midday. The highway was deserted except for a sixteen-wheeler in the center lane. The sign on the rear of the silver trailer came into focus. "If you can't see my mirror, I can't see you," it read. "Uh-oh," Lila grunted. She increased her speed. Just then, a doe ran out of the woods. Here comes the buck, she smiled to herself. After all, it is rutting season. Suddenly, to her horror, the heavy trailer was swinging into her path. She floored the gas again and swerved to avoid it, but the trailer caught her car's rear end. They were airborne! Lila held her breath.

The car jolted to a stop on the stump of a tree, hanging there lopsided. Her terror-filled thoughts dictated, "Escape now!" Carefully she leaned toward the passenger side door; it flew open. Inching herself under the steering wheel, she dropped to the ground. Her baby in the backseat was screaming. Lila, eyes wide with fright, wrenched open the rear door, unfastened the belt of the car seat, and clutching her screaming child, grabbed the two duffel bags that were beside her and staggered away from the now teetering car.

Seconds later, it rolled down the embankment and began sliding through the woods. Cradling her baby, Lila staggered a few yards. Her legs were shaking. Dropping the two bags, she sank down in the mass of leaves. The child was whimpering, "Mama, Mama."

"We'll rest here a minute, Chloe. It's all right. We're safe." She could not run any further until her muscles stopped vibrating. The car was careening through the sloping woods. She could not see the edge of the precipice. The car disappeared. It plunged over, falling into the gorge below. The sound of the crash cracked the silence of the woods, and then the boom of the explosion sent a lick of flame into the air.

"My God," Lila groaned. "That could have been us in there. We were inches from death." She breathed deeply, trying to calm herself. Her back was stiff with pain. The child, protected by a puffy snowsuit, seemed okay.

I've got to get out of here, she told herself, pain or no. Still shaky, she rose and stumbled along through the woods. A distance ahead she saw the roof of a rest-stop restaurant. She picked her way slowly, trying not to trip on branches while calming the crying child in her arms. She cooed to her, "Hush, Chloe baby, everything will be fine. See, we're coming out of the woods. See the red roof, darling. Hush now."

She trudged toward a baggage cart in the rest-stop parking lot, dumping the two duffels into it. They made first for the rest room. With no one near, she dared to push the wagon inside. Her hands shook as she checked Chloe's little limbs and her chest. Chloe smiled at the attention, and Lila felt her blood pressure go down when she realized her child escaped injury. She put a fresh diaper on Chloe and then set her on the counter with her juice box. Steadying her with one hand, she tried to wash her own face using the other. She put her fingers through her curly hair, matted on her forehead. With a paper towel she dried her face and saw in the mirror a distraught woman, her mouth open, her eyes staring, looking back at her like Munch's *The Scream*. Gently, she swabbed the tears on her child's face. I have to get myself together, she thought. I must think what to do next.

Mother and child sat down at a table in the nearly deserted restaurant. Who was here at this ungodly hour? It was 5:00 a.m. She had been crazy to travel so long. She should have put in at a motel after supper, whether sleepy or not.

Lila called to a passing busboy. "Please, take this and bring me a black coffee and a sweet roll." The teen took the five dollars and loped to the counter. Now calmer, Lila thought, No one would ever believe we survived that crash. Gymnastics training paid off big-time today. That means I am actually free, free of the devil. I don't ever have to see that man again. I don't have to go through a divorce with him staring at me or threatening to kill me. He'll never find me. He won't care that we are gone. He so much as told me to disappear. She closed her eyes, thinking about the daring idea of hiding from him, and a thrill went through her.

Chloe laughing in her ear roused her from her wild thoughts. The busboy was making funny faces for the child, and she giggled in her delightful musical voice. He plunked down the coffee, a plate with a jelly donut, a dollar and some change. "Keep it," said the woman. "I'm grateful to you. One second, do any buses stop here?"

"The buses are parked on that side," he said, pointing to the far lot. The woman nodded, sipping her coffee and breaking off a piece of the bun for her child. Somewhat recovered and excited about her prospects of being free, she made her way to the bus park. The buses' destinations were on the front panel above the windshields. A driver was lounging with his coffee next to a bus marked "Pittsburgh." Several passengers were asleep in the seats.

"I'd like to board please," Lila said.

"We don't pick up passengers here," the driver mumbled.

"Please, this is a special circumstance. I'll pay whatever the ticket costs for us from your last stop, just please let me on." The driver frowned, but seeing the mother, a duffel hanging from each shoulder, and the child, he relented. Probably got into a fight with her boyfriend, he imagined. Well, he knew how that could be. He opened the door and let her in.

"Take a seat in the back. No one's seated back there. I'm leaving shortly," he said, pocketing the cash she gave him. She sat Chloe down, stowed her bags, and fell into the plush covered seat with a sigh of relief.

The day before the crash, Lila Leif Ostro drew out all but a thousand dollars of her savings from the bank. She was fleeing her husband. It had been a horrible marriage. She had made a terrible mistake. But now it was over, and she was free of it. She had fifteen thousand dollars in cash in a six-pack bag stashed under her clothes in the duffel, money she had saved from her teacher's salary.

Her plan had been to drive to a town near where her brother lived, find an efficiency apartment and a lawyer, and file for divorce. Her brother had a houseful of five children. She could not depend on him for housing, but he would be a comfort and Chloe would have cousins to visit. Since he was a principal in a middle school, he might be able to get her a job. That plan was out the window now. If she were to become some other person, she could not contact him, not right away at any rate.

The bus sped along the highway. Chloe was asleep in her arms. She smiled at her child. I have this wonderful person from my dreadful marriage. She's my anchor. Smiling at the thought, she dozed. The bus stopped, waking her. It was daylight. A few passengers boarded. Whew, she breathed, what's next? No matter what, I must have a car. Now she scanned the road, passing a string of used car places as the sun rose higher. Her brother's home was in the outskirts of Pittsburgh. She didn't want to go that far. A half-hour later the bus was slowing again. She saw a sign, Car Mall.

"Getting off," she said aloud impulsively. "Getting off, driver!" She retrieved her bags, zipped up Chloe's snowsuit, and inching her way down the aisle, left the bus with several other passengers. The driver was doing his paperwork. He didn't look up.

As soon as she entered the lot, a rotund salesman approached her, morning coffee in hand. He listened to her needs and helped her find a car for six thousand dollars that he promised was roadworthy.

"I have a kid too. I wouldn't let you buy a car I wouldn't ride in," he said. Since it was a cash transaction, she had gotten a good deal, he assured her.

On the paperwork, she thought quickly. She gave her name as Lila Bronstein. She explained that she had never changed it on her license when she got married. Where did she get the name Bronstein? She must have seen it somewhere along the road. "I need a car seat," she told the salesman. He produced a used one and said he'd throw it in. "We always try to keep one handy. This is the best of the lot." Lila asked where she might find a children's store and was told that a few miles down the road was the town of St. George that had everything in a strip mall "and more stores on the main drag." He kissed Lila lightly on the cheek, and she smiled. She was on her way.

She drove until she saw a motel sign. The desk clerk nodded when she asked if they had a high chair and a crib. She registered as Lila Bronstein, pausing to be sure that was the name she had given for her car. In the motel room, she bathed and dressed Chloe, singing to her. Then the two walked around the motel, examining the leaves of a maple tree and listening to frogs croaking in a nearby pond. She bought a takeout dinner at the restaurant next door to the motel. Chloe held her hand, taking her baby steps back to their room. The child opened her mouth happily as Lila spooned some bottled toddler food for her. Chloe drank from her sippy cup, and then her eyes drooped. Lila gently placed her in the crib.

With Chloe peacefully asleep, Lila devoured her now tepid omelet. She looked into the crib. "You've had a horrible time, sweetheart," she whispered. "Your nutty mother is taking you on an unknown path, but it'll be better than what we had."

The thought of Alton made her shiver. She'd keep her survival to herself. At least for a while, she decided. She needed space to sort out her feelings. Would he come after her if she contacted him? He went ballistic when she suggested divorce. It would be another failure for him. Or would he now rejoice to learn he was rid of both her and the child and the problems they caused him? The man was so unstable it was hard to predict what he would do.

How could I have been so stupid, so blind? He seemed so pleasant at first; he was admired at the university, their star professor. I had doubts, but I let ambition get in the way. And face it, I was envious of Judith. I wanted a home and children. I was like a forgotten shell of an abandoned boat. I felt empty. I wanted to belong to someone, a person who cared for me.

She was near tears with no one to console her. It's hard to be alone, she admitted to herself. But she had been alone for the two years of their marriage, except for little Chloe.

"I'll keep you safe, my darling child," she whispered. Then she soaked in a hot bath, easing her spine, not climbing out until the water cooled. She fell into a deep sleep on the motel bed, waking with a start to the sound of a truck revving its motor outside. It was one o'clock. Chloe was still napping.

Lila had been dreaming of Alton; his shadow was still before her. Was it right to give up on the man she had wed? She rummaged in her duffel for a fresh T-shirt. Could I have done any more? She argued with herself. She put on the shirt. He didn't want to look inside himself or realize what damage he could do to others. He was brilliant and a sociopath—and that's being generous. She combed her hair before the mirror. I feel comfort in the anonymity of being a new person. Is that irresponsible? On the contrary, it's a win-win situation. It makes me feel so safe, so clean. I can do whatever I wish, and I have my baby too. It's so uncomplicated. I can just be me. So I better start thinking of what I should do in my new life.

Chapter 3

It was not like Lila Leif Ostro "Bronstein" to dissemble. She came from a family of freethinkers who were not afraid to oppose a trend that didn't square with their ideals. They eschewed any religion. Bill Leif thought religion a lot of bunk. He quickly challenged the notion of Santa Claus when Lila, age five, wanted to enter the roped-off area in the mall with a live Santa on the stage. Her parents believed in kindness, moral behavior, virtues that belonged to all mankind, and appreciation of nature. Her Aunt Mae attended the local church, but the Leifs would have none of that.

Lila Leif was an active youngster who never walked when she could run. At the town pool, she'd ask her brother to help her perfect her dives or her back flips on the lawn in front of their house. He was nine years older, and he felt protective of his little sister and encouraged her antics. Sometimes he'd complain.

"That's enough, Lila. Your legs are together. Now go play with your friends. You don't have to be perfect every time." She liked perfection though. It made her feel complete.

Their father was a mediator between management and labor at an automobile manufacturing site. Bill Leif, a jovial beer-drinking fellow, affected working-class manners although he was a graduate of the Cornell University School of Labor Relations and had been successful in negotiations that avoided strikes. The union liked him when contracts went their way. When it didn't, some hotheads could cause trouble.

One night, when she was eight, Lila was awakened by yelling in the street outside their stucco-clad home. She peeked out from her second story window and looked below. Ten men were clustered on the sidewalk; several were throwing eggs at the house. Lila wanted to laugh, but the men looked mean to her and she was frightened. She ran to her parents' room.

"Oh, Lila, I'm so sorry you were startled up," her mother said, embracing her. "It's just guys letting off steam. Dad will handle it, don't worry, sweetheart."

"Why do they look so angry? And why waste all those eggs?"

Her mother laughed. "Silly, isn't it? Grown men. I don't know the problem, but your father has made some arrangements for them at work they probably don't like. He'll take care of it. See, it's quieted down."

They could hear the door opening downstairs. There was the sound of tramping feet. She looked at her mother.

"Your father, he's invited them in for a beer, I'll bet." The mother looked out. The master bedroom was in the back of the house, but from a corner window she could see the street.

"See, Lila, most of them are going home. The rest will be laughing in the kitchen in a moment. You can go to sleep, dear. Dad will explain the new work rules to them and what they got in return. Then they will go home too."

The next morning, the door was wet from the hosing down her father gave it.

"What's this?" asked Martin, as water dripped on his sleeve while they were leaving for school.

"Martin," Lila chided him, "you slept through all these crazy men throwing eggs at our house."

Martin, a high school senior, shrugged. He remembered incidents before this one. Their mother always explained that people sometimes became angry but that there was goodness in all people; you just had to find it. "Your daddy is a specialist at that," she'd say smiling. Grace Leif once confided that the businessmen in town only spoke to her husband when there was tension in the plant over some matter and they needed him to side with them. "But your dad is always fair, that's his guiding principle," she told her children.

It gave her a bad feeling inside to see that her father was disrespected. It made her angry, but she didn't know how to focus her anger. It's just that she wanted respect for her parents and for herself and Martin.

Lila did her homework at the little desk in her room upstairs. She was writing out the spelling words of the week, but each time she made a mistake on the page, she crumpled it up and started over. Then she saw she had spelled *They* with an *a*. She was furious with herself and tore that paper up too and threw it in the wastebasket. She must have let out a groan because her mother tapped on the door.

"Are you okay in there?" Grace said.

"I keep making mistakes!" she shouted. "I want a perfect paper."

"You can erase," her mother said coming in. "Why not erase instead of starting over each time?" Grace looked at the crumpled sheets of paper in the wastebasket. "Your teacher will think more of you when she sees that you know how to correct your mistakes."

"I like it perfect," the child said. Grace shrugged.

"That's good if not carried to extremes, Lila. Extremes are not good in anything." She'll grow out of it, Grace thought to herself.

"To be kind to people, you don't need deities to tell you what to do" was another of her mother's beliefs. As a youngster, Lila could see the Christmas lights and wreaths decorating houses on her street. There was excitement in the air at that season. In her friend Alice's house, there was a glorious tree with spangles and fragile little balls. She helped Alice with the decorations one week before Christmas. She saw how lovingly her friend took the colorful balls from the box where they had rested all year waiting for the annual ritual. Lila would carefully hand one ball at a time up to Alice on a ladder until all the balls were hung. The two girls would admire the tree. Then Lila would go home to her comfortable but unadorned house, close the door, and pull down the shade in her room that faced the street.

Martin left for college that year. He was a freshman at the University of Michigan, and she missed him. Her mother, Grace, who worked in a doctor's office, wouldn't be home until six. Sometimes her Aunt Mae came to keep her company, but mostly she was alone in the house until dinner time. She'd set the table and read her young adult novel or do her homework.

When they were eating dinner, Lila asked a question. "Are we Jewish?"

"What makes you ask that?" Grace said.

"Because Alice said that's why we don't celebrate Christmas or have a wreath or anything."

"It's true that Jews don't celebrate the holiday because it represents the birth of Jesus, the Messiah, and Jews don't believe he was the Messiah."

"And if you want to see how silly this all is, Lila," her father said, wiping his mouth and putting down his fork, "Jesus was a Jew."

"So aren't Jews happy he was born?" Lila persisted.

"I'm sure his parents were happy when he was born," Grace said. "Jews don't think he was the Messiah, that's all."

"What is a messiah, anyway?" the girl asked.

"Grace, you tell her. I'm eating my supper."

"Messiah is a personage who can save mankind. And that can lead to a million more questions that are hard to answer simply. We don't believe in a messiah, but we are not Jewish. Jews do celebrate their right to worship at Hanukkah. They put a light in their window. Last week it was Hanukkah. Now it's almost Christmas. People have all these myths about their celebrations. We don't go along with this thinking. It just divides people. Now, Lila, please help me clear."

"Well, I would like to have a wreath on the door or put lights in the window. So there!" Lila shot back, perturbed that her family was not connected to any celebrations besides Earth Day.

She felt a yearning for something more, but she didn't know where to look. That spring, her yearning found a focus.

She was nine-going-on-ten and doing cartwheels on the lawn while Alice tried to copy her, crumbling in midair and laughing. A high school coach who lived down the block stood by to watch. He called to Lila to come closer.

"Young lady, I think you have the perfect build and flexibility to be a gymnast," he said. "If you like tumbling, I think you'd like my beginners' gymnastics class. Would that interest you?"

Lila's eyes widened. She nodded. She wasn't sure what gymnasts did, but she told her parents about the offer at dinner. They knew Coach Little and invited him over. Grace Leif didn't want Lila walking the seven blocks to their house alone at dusk. The coach took several kids home after practice; when he offered to include Lila in his run, her parents gave their consent.

Chapter 4

Lila's whole world changed in that class. She delighted in following the coach's directions and felt a new strength and sureness in her body as she completed one maneuver after another. She acquired an identity; she was a gymnast! She also learned something about herself. She hated to have a less-than-perfect exercise. If she didn't land with both feet at the same time, if she wobbled jumping from the trampoline, she was upset. Coach Little told her to take it easy. She was doing fine, but he admired her goal of perfection. She hated a sloppy execution, and gradually she perfected the moves.

Lila reveled in a sport that allowed her to travel to other schools for competitions and to other cities when she was on the high school team. Swinging on the bars, gaining speed, letting go and catching the opposite bar gave her a supreme feeling of freedom and power. Completing rotations and landing squarely on both feet when she flipped from the beam gave her the pleasure that comes from the mastery of a skill. During competitions, her mother would sit in the stands holding her breath. The two would grin at each other when she completed a perfect set.

Once, during a competition, she had points deducted from her performance that she felt was unfair. She wanted to complain to the judges, but Coach Little held her back.

"They are only human," he said. "Sometimes they miss an error in a gymnast's favor. It's part of the game. You have to let it go, Lila. You scored well."

"They should know their mistakes," she replied. "They should be fair." The coach sighed and shrugged.

Lila became a leading gymnast in high school, and when the school won a regional competition, she was awarded a plaque and a statue. Not wishing to take credit above the others, she accepted the honor on behalf of her whole team, but she was pleased nonetheless for the applause that greeted her. When you strive for perfection, you are rewarded, she told herself, and the fairness of it made her smile.

When she was chosen to be queen of the prom with a boastful football player as her king, she hesitated. The drawback for Lila was that Stephan, the football captain with his big body and big square teeth, would be her designated escort. Her friends urged her to take the honor. They had voted for her, they said. Only the first dance belonged to him; after that, she was free to dance with whoever asked her. She admitted to herself that being Prom Queen gave her a certain feeling of power. It would please her parents too. She accepted.

All the girls were buying dresses for the prom, and Lila found one in a bridal shop. It had a black skirt and a pink and black lattice pattern on top with spaghetti-thin silk straps at the shoulders. When Lila paraded in front of her mother before the dance, Grace smiled and wiped her eyes. "You look so lovely," she said. "I don't know how a plain-looking couple as your dad and I produced such a beautiful girl!"

Lila didn't care that she was thought of as pretty. It wasn't something she earned on her own, so she took no pride in it.

On the night of the prom, Stephan called for her in his two-door sports car by beeping the horn. That didn't sit well with Bill Leif, football star or not.

"Get in here, boy," he yelled at the door, holding it open until Stephan lumbered out of the car with a florist's box in his hand. Grace pinned the flower to her daughter's gown.

"You both look special," she said smiling. "Have a good time."

It was an exhausting night. Lila danced every dance and took part in various ceremonies until the band played its last notes. Happy but pleased with herself, she now had to deal with Stephan.

"Let's go," said he. "Now the real fun starts."

Lila frowned. She was ready to go home. "Stephan, you'll drive me home, please. I really don't want to go to a party. I'm dead tired, and I have my gym practice in the morning."

Stephan shrugged. "Okay, darlin', if that's the way you want it—the car will do fine." They got in, Lila sitting primly in the passenger seat. But Stephan headed in the opposite direction toward a wooded area near the school. She was about to object when Stephen slowed the car and said in a concerned voice, "Listen, Lila, would you look in the backseat a minute. I might have left my wallet there." Annoyed but feeling this request was hard to dismiss, she craned her neck and said she didn't see anything. "Well, please, let's get you a good look back there." They both got out of the car, and Stephan moved the front passenger seat forward so Lila, with her long dress, could peek into the car.

"I don't see anything, Stephan," she said.

"Go in further, it might be behind my seat." Sighing, Lila swiveled inside. At that moment, Stephan flung himself upon her.

"What are you doing, Stephan? Get off me!" she yelled.

"Every king on prom night claims his queen, didn't know that, baby?" He began groping under the hem of her dress with one hand and fondling her breast with another.

"Stephan, stop this!" She pressed on his shoulders with both hands and turned her face from side to side as he tried to kiss her. "Monster!" she spat out through muffled lips.

Squirming away from him, Lila kneed the man with all her strength. He rolled away holding himself in pain. "Bitch, you bitch," he called.

Lila braced her body and launched herself over the front seat and out the door! Breathing heavily, she stumbled down the street holding up her skirt, gritting her teeth in anger. She ducked between the houses beyond the woods to a street that wound around to her house a half-mile away. The car didn't follow her. She staggered along in the dark, breathing hard, close to a sob. One more block and she saw her house. She opened her front door slowly and, holding her shoes in her hand, crept up the steps to her room. Her parents slept on. She rolled up her dress and stuffed it in a trash bag, pushing it into her closet. She threw her underpants in the garbage downstairs and took a shower, scrubbing herself over and over, angry and cursing all the while. She lay on the bed, fury making her turn from side to side and flip her body up and down in exasperation. She only calmed herself when she resolved to report Stephan's attack to the football coach. Finally, exhausted, Lila curled up into a ball and fell asleep.

She called Coach Little on Sunday morning, begging off from practice. "Too much prom?" he said with a chuckle.

"Too much," Lila echoed briefly. On Monday, she strode into Reggie Tanner's office, the football coach. She accused Stephan of attacking her in the backseat of his car after the prom.

The coach listened with a wry smile. "Ah," he said. "Boys will be boys. You know how it is, the testosterone flows and my boys get a little wild."

"He assaulted me, Coach. Are you excusing this behavior?" Lila asked, her eyes flashing.

"Well, now, sweetie, if you're not physically hurt . . ."

Lila shook her head in disbelief. The man shrugged, and the two sat and glared at each other.

"I'll take a pass to the principal's office," she said firmly. The coach filled out a form and handed it to her, narrowing his eyes. Lila rose, turned her back on him, and stalked out of his office.

The principal, a stiff, proper gentleman, listened. He asked if she had told her parents. She said no; she was too ashamed. Her real reason was that her parents, though sympathetic, would try to make her understand the boy's side and ask her to make friends with him. She couldn't bear to hear any of that kind of thinking, and so she would never learn if they would have done differently. It was her problem; no need to have parents involved.

The principal shook his head after hearing her tale. "Let's have you speak to Mrs. Malcolm. Do you know her?" Lila nodded. He pressed a button on his phone and exchanged a few words Lila couldn't hear. "Mrs. Malcolm will meet you in the teacher's lounge," the principal smiled, "and here is a pass for your next class."

Mrs. Malcolm, one of the vice principals, was a sympathetic older woman. After listening to Lila's account of her prom night horror, and seeing Lila's angry eyes, she had one question: "Was there penetration?" Lila said no.

"Well, then, you've had an ugly experience. Try to see it for what it was. You shoved him off. That showed pluck. Good for you. Best forget it, dear, and carry on."

"That's it. You are not going to discipline Stephan?"

"We'll talk to him, you can be sure."

"I see," Lila said, looking the woman in the eye.

"Now, dear," Mrs. Malcolm said, alarmed. "It's only days from graduation. We don't want to upset the plans of the parents and our students who have worked so hard all these years. Both of you have exemplary records. Please put this unpleasantness away and enjoy yourself. Lila, are you okay with that?"

"No," Lila said boldly. "But to save my parents anguish, I'll shut up, which is what you all want me to do!" She stood and looked at the woman, who offered a weak smile. Lila turned and walked out of the lounge.

At graduation, she barely touched hands with the principal and took her diploma from Mrs. Malcolm with a frozen face. She cringed when she saw the principal give Stephan's hand a hearty shake and gritted her teeth when Mrs. Malcolm let Stephan hug her.

Her mother had noticed her cold reaction on the stage, and when they were reunited after the graduation ceremony, she asked, "Is there anything wrong, Lila? You don't look happy, dear. Why is that? It's a happy day."

Lila smiled at her mother who wanted all people to love each other. She had gotten over the trauma of the evening. The infuriating episode wouldn't hold her back, but she'd never forget the disdain with which the school heads had treated her sorry story.

Chapter 5

The coach at a small women's college in upstate New York with a strong athletic program had offered Lila a scholarship and a chance to compete on the school gymnast team. Lila had been accepted at Michigan State and had been trying to decide between the two schools. Now her mind was made up. Lila opted for the small school.

At college, she felt a certain freedom in the all-women classes where each student had a chance to shine. She loved the courses in psychology and philosophy and the different theories of how true education could best be achieved. She felt a responsibility to learn all she could. At the same time, she loved the physical satisfaction of working on her skills in gymnastics, retaining the suppleness and flexibility she had since her early teens.

Lila and teammate Judith Mayer became fast friends. Judith had a sturdy frame and muscles toned by years of gymnastics. She wove her jet-black hair into a bun for the sport. She had full lips and dark eyes with luxurious lashes to match

Lila at eighteen was taller and slimmer than Judith. Her light-brown hair had been curly as a youngster and now had a natural wave. She kept it short for gymnastics. Lila had more delicate features and a small straight nose. The curve of her lips and her wide gray-green eyes lit up her face when she smiled. If something displeased her, she narrowed her eyes and wrinkled her brow, assuming a severe look that demanded attention. It was a look that her future students learned to avoid.

Judith was a home economics major and a good cook. She and Lila would concoct meals in the dorm kitchen from simple ingredients that Judith made delicious through her use of spices Lila never had experienced at home. Lila was scrupulous in cleaning up the kitchen after and wouldn't stop until it was spotless.

"What's with you?" Judith complained. "You're cleaning up other people's mess. It's clean enough, let's go."

"I don't know. I can't go until everything is shining. You go ahead."

"No, I'll wait. But I'm warning you, I'm dragging you out when the clock strikes twelve!"

Lila decided to major in early childhood education. The field trips to local schools to observe young students excited her imagination. The deeper she got into education techniques and philosophies, the more she was confirmed that this was to be her field, a place where she could make a difference in the lives of young children. A good preschool education could set a student on the right path for future learning. She wasn't interested in teaching the higher grades. She wanted to be there at the beginning.

The girls at her college never lacked for weekend dates because there were several men's colleges in the area. Lila met a slim, studious, shy guy from a technical school with whom she had good conversations and who was slow to ask for intimacies. She felt safe with him and found she enjoyed his kisses. When she called a halt before things got out of hand, this boy respected her enough to stop.

At the end of a successful sophomore year, Lila bounced home feeling good about herself and her future. She looked forward to working in a local Y day camp for the summer. Instead, her father met her at the airport with dismaying news.

Her parents had kept from her that her mother, Grace, was gravely ill, diagnosed with stage-four cancer. Lila spent the summer at her mother's side, making her comfortable, driving her to treatments, and performing the household tasks. She loved taking care of her mother. She had little free time for herself, but she had no regrets. By September, Grace Leif was under hospice care. Lila held her hand as she faded away.

There was to no one to lead at the graveside funeral. Lila stepped forward to speak. She praised her mother's goodness and, holding back tears, said she loved her dearly and would miss her. The president of the Audubon Society said that Grace's devotion to nature was an inspiration. She recalled how Grace always volunteered for the bird count twice each year, in cold or heat, and kept the best records. Her father spoke a few words, then choked up and tossed a rose onto the casket. They went back to their house and sat with a few friends. Lila felt lost. Martin tried to comfort her. She told her Aunt Mae, "Just to put a life away in the earth seems such an abrupt ending for such an important person as my mother was. I wish I had known about her illness before, so I could have been with her longer."

"Now, honey, your mother was happy you were in school and did not want you called home."

"Still, I wish I had been given the choice."

Lila offered to remain in Flint and keep house for her father, but he wouldn't hear of it.

"You finish school. You have your life to live. Besides, Doreen Shultz has offered to come in and look to my needs.

I'll be all right." So Lila returned to college for her junior year and she was not too surprised to learn, at Christmas break, that her father and Doreen would marry.

Chapter 6

Lila and Judith were odd ducks among their classmates who talked only of getting jobs in New York City and having careers. Lila and Judith were family-oriented. In the age of Women's Lib, Judith expected to work in the lab for a wholesale food manufacturer where the Rush University was located and Lila to teach, but both believed their main goal was having a family life with a capable husband and children to love. Judith's boyfriend, Harvey, a few years older than Judith and Lila, was in his last year in the College of Optometry at Rush. When he graduated, he planned to join a practice in the university town, and after Judith's graduation, there would be a grand wedding.

Spring break was coming up. Lila wasn't enamored of her father's wife and mentioned her reluctance to go back to Michigan for the recess. Judith said she would be thrilled to have her stay with her family, who had a large brick house in Utica.

"The only hitch is you'll have to go through our family Seder. It's Passover, and we have this special meal with readings and all. After that, we'll join our local gang of college kids and hang out."

Although Lila had stayed at the Mayers' house before, she discovered that the Seder was a formal meal with many guests. She'd have to give it her full attention so as not to seem out of place. There was an extension on the already large table in the dining room. Mr. Mayer's overweight business partner and his wife and their two young children were introduced. Judith's girl cousins came over from the state university. They seemed aloof but perked up when Harvey greeted them. At the head of the table was Judith's grandfather, his gray head bobbing as he murmured words from a prayer book. Lila was seated next to Judith, and to Judith's left was jolly Harvey, the love of her life who would spend the second Seder with his own family. They all welcomed Lila with smiles and handshakes.

Lila found the Seder fascinating. In the center of the table was a large plate with little dishes on it. Each had a mysterious assortment of items, an egg, a bone, and some veggies. A cloth embroidered with the word *matzos* hid large, flat square crackers. On each of Mrs. Mayer's white china plates was a small book from which the guests took turns reading. Jessica, the partner's little girl, sang Hebrew words to a long passage dubbed the "Four Questions." Everyone applauded when she had finished. When her turn came, Lila carefully read a passage. As the readings progressed, the meaning of the egg and veggies became clear.

As an education major, she thought the Haggadah and the symbolic vegetables and matzos that were part of the story a fabulous way to tell the children—and, to be truthful, herself—the tale of freedom from Pharaoh and the cruelties of slavery. She doubted that the miracle of the parting of the sea took place but that the Seder was a magical way to convey universal ideas of freedom and courage. It was the most unusual meal she ever had and quite wonderful, she thought, wistfully wishing that as a child she had been part of it.

"To the doubters around the table, miracles do happen," Judith's father proclaimed as if he could read her thoughts. He glanced at the cousins who had shrugged and whispered together during the reading of the parting of the sea. "You may question the miracle of the Sea of Reeds opening up for the Israelites to cross, but think about it, in 1967, wasn't it a miracle that the outnumbered Israelis defeated the massed armies of Egypt, Jordan, and Syria? And in six days! Who will believe that a century from now except to say it was a miracle?" Then smiling, he declared—"Discuss!"

The cousins debated Harvey, one another, and the grandfather, who said, "It doesn't have to be true to be believed."

"Grandpa, you're saying have a little faith." Judith sung the last words.

Judith's mother called for order. "The dinner is waiting, children." They bent their heads to read the little book, up to the words "The meal is served."

"Hurrah!" called Harvey. A platter of hard-boiled eggs was passed around to be dipped into each person's tiny dish of salted water. Matzo was spread with a mixture of chopped apples, nuts, and wine. Judith and Lila began carefully bringing in plates of shimmering broth with a round matzo ball in the center. The matzo was making a mess on the table, flakes of the cracker everywhere.

"Should we crumb?" Lila whispered to Judith.

"Nah, it's okay. We'll shake out the cloth later." Lila would have liked a neater table, but she let it go.

After the meal, the grandfather read the Hebrew in rapid-fire bursts, and then there were intriguing songs with the cousins singing with fervor. Lila was dazzled by it all. After singing each blessing that God bestowed on the Israelites, the group chorused, *"Diyanu!"* It would have been sufficient. After the second *diyanu,* Lila caught on and joined in, singing along happily.

A year later, the girls graduated. Her dad couldn't come to the graduation because of health issues, so Lila flew back home to Flint to see him. He presented her with a new green compact car. She was ecstatic to accept it and drove it back to her college town in August to take up her post in the public school where she had been a student teacher. She shared an apartment with a fellow teacher in the school, a dour single older woman with whom she had little in common. But her car gave her the freedom to travel about on weekends. She and Sally, another young teacher, visited New York City, took in a museum and a musical, and met with college friends who were working there. During the spring break, she and Sally flew to Paris and, following the advice of friends' recommendations, ate the most wonderful food she had ever tasted. They teamed up with two male graduate students from Washington State and traveled with them to Versailles and Longchamps. They passed a Roma camp, where Lila was appalled at the squalor in which little children lived. It saddened her that parents would not want to do better for their kids.

In May, she drove to Utica to be a bridesmaid at Judith and Harvey's wedding. She was introduced to the *chupah,* the wedding canopy, and the glass wrapped in paper that Harvey pounced on with glee. Everyone clapped and cheered. Harvey and Judith were hoisted up on chairs while the band played and guests sang. Lila was entranced by the ceremony. She watched the hora for a while and then joined in the dancing.

She felt a joy washing over her to be part of the celebration. Life-changing events should be marked by some special recognition, she thought, in contrast to her family's dislike of what they called artificially created happenings.

It was wonderful to see Judith so happy. Lila had a sinking feeling that the friendship she had enjoyed with Judith would fade away now that college was over. Though she was absorbed in her new role as a kindergarten teacher, Lila wondered what else life had in store for her. During college she had dates with men, but nothing serious had developed. There was no marriage to go to for her. Sometimes at night in her bed, she had a hollow feeling. Who was she? Who did she belong to? The answer was "no one." It was a fearful thought that she tried to banish from her mind. But in the darkness, when the excitement of the day had ended, it came back again and again.

Chapter 7

As her year at the local kindergarten came to an end, Lila poured over the want ads in the educators' newsletters. She felt her blood pressure soar when she saw a notice announcing a vacancy for a pre-K teacher in the Rush University's demonstration school. At once, she submitted her application, enclosing favorable letters from her teachers and the principal of the school where she taught. She raced home each day to look for the mail. She had no idea if she had a chance even though Judith said, "You'll get it. I'm sure of it."

A letter with the university logo was in her mailbox! She tore open the envelope. She felt warmth flushing her cheeks as she read the letter requesting an interview. She drove to the school determined to make a good impression. She was offered the job.

How wonderful, she thought. Now she could relocate to Judith and Harvey's larger town and remain in an academic setting where she could grow professionally. She'd begin taking classes for her master's degree.

Both girls had given up gymnastics after their junior year; neither was to be an Olympian. The former gymnasts were determined to keep their bodies in shape without the discipline of training. They had worked out and taken long runs together during college. Now with Lila near, they could resume their routine after work or on weekends.

Judith found Lila an apartment in an old mansion the landlady had turned into small apartment residences.

"You'll work out at the U gym," Judith said teasingly, "and I'll join you, at least for a couple of months."

Lila looked at her friend quizzically.

"I'm pregnant," Judith shouted, grinning. The two girls screamed joyously and embraced.

"Yeah, yeah," said Lila. "Count on me for a babysitter."

Six months later, when Nathan was born, Lila experienced the *brit milah,* his circumcision.

"Judith," she said, "I hope you have lots of boys, but you don't have to invite me to that ceremony again." They both laughed.

"But it's very important. That's one of the ways that makes a Jew a Jew, at least for the boys."

That was three years ago. Judith was pregnant again, and she woke Lila one Sunday morning to ask a favor. Harvey had to go into his optical store and couldn't take Nathan to his Sunday school class. Judith was feeling queasy; would Lila be so kind as to drive Nathan to the temple and wait the two hours that the class runs to take him back home?

Only too happy to help out, Lila not only took him to the class but sat in the back with her *New York Times Book Review* and listened to the kids practice, learning two of the three *bruchas,* recited before Friday night dinner. Little did she know how that tutorial would be helpful to her sometime in the future. She read sporadically, hearing the kids stumbling over the words and laughing at first and, finally, reciting together the blessing for bread and wine. "You did well, Nathan," she said smiling, walking him to her car. "Your parents will be proud of you."

Lila wondered how she would ever catch up to Judith. Although her work as a teacher was absorbing, she longed to find a man to love. She went on dates, but none of the men pleased her. Sometimes, she had a funny ache that she realized was fear, fear that she couldn't respond to men with any passion. Was she too fastidious? Did she think sex was messy? She laughed to herself—no, she liked sex.

She had dated a graduate student over the past year. It was a convenience for them both—no need to wonder what to do on a Saturday night. They enjoyed dinners together, him treating one week, her the next. On Sundays they joined the hiking club and explored the many trails in the Adirondack Mountains. Lila loved the cool clean air in the mountains and the views of forests and lakes. It felt so good to stretch her legs and leave the heated environment of campus life for a few hours each week.

Gary was a computer science nut, talking about how computers were going to dominate every field of endeavor and that the university was on the cutting edge. He urged Lila to take a master's in computers instead of education.

"How do you think our local genius, Professor Ostro, would be able to do his work on a unified theory if it wasn't for computer technology?" Gary challenged. Lila grinned at him, explaining patiently that Gary had his thing for machines, but she preferred to deal with little minds and help them grow.

They had both been experimenting with each other's sexuality, and she experienced pleasure in their contacts. She was relieved that she had no hang-ups over her miserable experience with her prom date. But when Gary went off to California for a job, he didn't ask her to come with him. She was somewhat miffed. She realized Gary had no deep interest in her. It left her feeling abandoned, even though he had never appealed to her as husband material. It was good-bye, Gary. She was twenty-five and alone.

Finding a lifetime mate is like a dance, she thought. You whirl around with this one and that one hoping to find a connection, someone in step with you. I'm weary of the dance. I'll just go solo for now. Maybe I'll be everyone's Aunt Lila, the old-maid schoolteacher. You can't let that happen, you silly duck, she laughed at herself. Still, she wondered if she had the capacity to love someone the way Judith loved Harvey.

Once a week, she had dinner with a fellow teacher who secretly wanted to be a chef. She loved Frederic's company; he was funny, smart, and gentlemanly, but it was nothing physical. They would go dutch treat to different restaurants each week where he analyzed every dish. Frederic sometimes wouldn't let her taste something until he described what its ingredients were first. She had her fork in the air, while he went on and on. "Frederic, you'll make me scream. Let's eat already." He teased Lila about a single male teacher at the school who had eyes for her but who did not interest her in the least.

"Don't encourage him," she warned Frederic.

Lila's pulse quickened at the university receptions that included faculty from the whole university family. The men and women were so worldly and intriguing. A distinguished professor from China was introduced to the throng one fall evening. He shook hands all around. She greeted him with pleasure. She was pleased he reached out to everyone in the room because otherwise she was almost ignored. The professors had their department heads around them or were speaking with other notables. Her role in university life was peripheral, she understood—a teacher in the demonstration school in the school of education. No one had tidbits to share with her until she spied her Lower School principal, a very tall woman in her fifties with long gray hair. Vera Sternberg smiled at her, and the woman's whole demeanor seemed to change.

Perhaps she is shy, Lila thought. Encouraged by her warm greeting, Lila walked over to her. She mentioned a misunderstanding at school that had a child in tears. A new boy in the kindergarten complained to his mother that all the other students were called by their first names while he alone was called by his last name, Blake. The mother came to the school to find out why. It turned out the office had recorded his name backward; he was Anderson Blake, not Blake Anderson.

"Young Anderson learned early to stand up for himself," Vera Sternberg said smiling.

"The kids don't call him Blake anymore, now they call him Andy," Lila grinned. "I hope that's all right with him. His teacher told me she is careful to call him Anderson." They both laughed pleasantly.

Soon, several other women, attracted by their banter, came over. Circulation in the room was like a moving stream, so when the dean of the physics department beckoned to her, Lila stepped aside from the group.

"I want you to meet someone who would like to meet you," Arthur Mayfield said invitingly. She let him guide her over to the famed Professor Alton Ostro of the physics faculty. They shook hands, and Dr. Mayfield backed away.

Alton Ostro asked if they could sit somewhere and talk. "Sure," she replied, slightly nervous before this distinguished man, a good deal older than she, wondering what he would want to talk to her about. They sat in a corner, apart from the throng. He asked about her job.

"The kids are a special group, very achieving, even at four years of age. Most of them are reading already—some self-taught, some promoted by involved parents. They are curious, attentive, ready for new challenges. I love them," she enthused.

"That's good," he said. "It's good to love your work. I love my work too. Too much so, says Arthur Mayfield. Can I walk you home soon?"

"I have my car. I live a bit away from the campus."

"Tomorrow there's a violinist playing in the black box theater. I'll get a ticket if you will join me."

"I'd like that," Lila said. "Shall I meet you there?"

"Yes, please. I have no car. I bike to the U. Come early, and we'll have dinner in the Commons," Ostro said.

Lila's heart was beating fast. Could this man really be interested in her? She'd have to call Judith first thing in the morning. Alton, as he asked her to call him, did get her heart racing.

Judith was impressed. "He must really like you! And why not? You're gorgeous and smart. He's famous. I'm thrilled for you. Harvey wants to know when we can double-date. I don't know if a simple doctor of optometry can measure up to a distinguished physicist, but he's excited about meeting him."

"Wait, Judy. It's just a first date. Maybe it'll be the last."

But it wasn't. At dinner, Ostro tried to explain his work for her, the quest for a grand unified theory that blended the force of gravity with three interactions. He drew a spiral on a napkin and explained that cosmic waves of energy are the basis for all matter. He went on describing his theory and how it differed from the String Theory, but he lost her after a few sentences with concepts that were alien to her as the Star Wars series that she had never watched.

She admitted her lack of knowledge of the sciences to him and wished instead he'd talk about his personal life. Had he ever been married? No, he never had, but he'd thought about it. He looked into her eyes. He asked about her family. Her mother was dead, and her father had remarried. He lived in Michigan where she and her brother grew up. Martin, her older brother, lived in Pittsburgh in a second marriage in a blended family—hers, his, and theirs, five kids in all. Alton nodded his acknowledgment. She didn't know whether he approved or was put off by such a family.

Ostro was an only child. His father had died when he was young. He grew up in his grandparents' home, and his mother wandered off after a while. He never heard from her again, even when his grandparents died. He had scholarships through college and earned his doctorate at twenty-four. He'd been at the university since then, fifteen years. He said all this without emotion. Just the facts, ma'am, she thought, amused. She knew he had authored scientific papers that brought him grants to do the work in which he had made a name for himself. The university was proud to have him.

Seated at the concert, Alton explained that he loved music. At least they had that in common. They both were moved by the violinist's virtuosity. Alton took her hand during the Brahms concerto, and she felt a thrill run through her. If he had wanted to kiss her right then and there, she would have responded. After the concert, he walked her to her car proposing that they spend Sunday together—a walk, a bike ride, a picnic maybe? She agreed.

She didn't tell Judith about the date. She wanted Alton to herself, to learn more about him. If Sunday worked out, there would be time enough for a double date. Judith's husband, Harvey, could be a bit overpowering with his heartiness.

Alton called at noon on Sunday. He said he had slept late, and could they meet at two o'clock? So much for a picnic. She ate the picnic lunch herself and then drove over to the U where Alton had two bikes ready. They rode away from the campus, up into the hills, and set the bikes down overlooking a small lake.

"It's beautiful up here, so serene," Lila said, gazing at the placid lake surrounded by maples resplendent in their fall yellows and reds. Alton had a rolled-up blanket on the back of his bike. They spread it on a grassy patch and squatted down, taking in the sun on this mild fall day. Alton picked up two fallen branches and began stripping away the leaves.

"I'd like to work with my hands someday," he said pensively. "I don't have the time now. But I believe in living simply. Basic needs should be satisfied but no frills. What do you need? A table, a chair, a bed. Someday, in a far-off time, I'd like to build these things we take for granted and live the simple life."

"A jug of wine, a loaf of bread, and thou!" Lila interjected, smiling.

"Exactly," he said, smiling back. "I wish I had thought to bring the wine. But we have the thou, I do hope." He leaned toward her. They kissed tentatively. She gazed at Alton's face. He had a slightly aquiline nose and deep-set eyes. He was not handsome, but his intensity excited her. Alton was tall, but he was so spare it looked like he hadn't had a good meal in years. She guessed that was just his nature as he ate with gusto in the college commons.

He tossed away the branches and took Lila's hand in his. His fingers were long and tapered. She felt a thrill once more as he bent to kiss her again, and she responded with a passion she had never experienced before. Was this the love she had been seeking? They kissed until they were out of breath and pulled apart. He didn't attempt to go further, for which she was grateful.

Could this man really be interested in a long-term relationship with someone who had such an ordinary mind? The next statement from him took her aback.

"I know it's soon, Lila," he said. "My intentions are very serious, though. If you would have me, I'd like to make you my wife."

"Oh, Alton," she whispered. "I don't know what to say." Her stomach was churning. What to say to him? After a moment, she spoke. "I'm very flattered, Alton. I feel an excitement I've never experienced before. Oh, my, I feel like . . . I don't want to discourage you, but it's so soon, sir. You don't really think I could keep up with you—I mean, intellectually."

"That's good. I don't want competition in my life. Just some peace. If you'll consider marriage, we'll go on from there. I wanted you to know where I stand is all."

She put her hand on his cheek, feeling the stubble on his haphazardly shaved face. Suddenly she felt motherly toward him, the brilliant boy who had been abandoned by his mother and was looking desperately for love. The difference in age and intellect disappeared for her in that moment. Her natural sense of self-protection, however, made her decide to proceed slowly. It was a little crazy to propose to a virtual stranger. Last week she was worrying that no man wanted her, and now this outstanding man was actually proposing. Unbelievable! She was excited by the possibilities, but she needed to know him better, another date or two, and then she'd call in Judith and Harvey.

Chapter 8

Date number three was a visit to Alton's house. He lived in a rented furnished colonial near the university. It was a nicely proportioned house, a bit dated but livable, except for one failing—it was in total disarray. "Alton," Lila said gently, "you have to get someone in to thoroughly clean this house. Not just straighten it up. It's not good for you to live this way, dust and papers all over."

Oh, I hope he's not sloppy, she thought. I couldn't stand that. The thought passed quickly.

"You're right," he said sheepishly. "I should have had it done before showing it to you. This is where we would live." After they got through that rough spot, they had a nice brunch in town and saw a foreign film. Sitting in her car in front of the house when she drove him home, they discussed the film. He didn't seem to understand the woman's motivation at all, and she laughed at him and called him a male chauvinist. He agreed she was probably right and asked her to come in. But she demurred, kissing him through the window. He walked up the path to his door without looking back. "Remember," she called out. "Thoroughly." He nodded at the door and went inside.

Lila and Alton called for the Goldsteins on their first double date. Harvey insisted that they come in while he did the Havdalah service. "It's only five minutes. We mark the end of the Sabbath by lighting the candle and smelling the spices." Alton shrugged. Lila was intrigued. She'd never seen a braided candle with three wicks before, and the ceremony was lovely. Nathan passed around a filigree tower of silver that contained spices. Each one took a whiff holding the tower close. The pleasant pungent odor tickled Lila's nose. Alton backed away when it was his turn. The candle was snuffed out.

"A good week to all," shouted the ebullient Harvey, echoed by Judith and Nathan. "Okay, let's go."

Harvey was blown away by Alton, he told Lila and Judith after the date. "He's on the cutting edge of a major leap in our understanding of the universe. It's very earthshaking what he's doing. It becomes an obsession, that kind of exploration. Your mind is working on it every waking moment when you're in it. That's how it is with him. It's like the Kabbalah. You're not supposed to study Kabbalah before you're forty, did you know that? And you have to be married because it takes possession of you. It can make you crazy. You need the maturity to know when to stop and smell the roses. I think Alton has that intensity."

Lila laughed. "Is that why he wants to marry me?"

"He does seem rather otherworldly," Judith said frowning. "I don't know that he'll be a lot of fun, Lila. And is he orderly? You know what a bug you are on neatness."

"Heck, Judy, not everyone gets a chance to live with a mind like Alton's. Don't discourage, Lila."

"Oh, you just want to say you are tight with Dr. Ostro. Tell your Op Society friends." He laughed; Lila just smiled. She wouldn't share that Alton's house had been a mess. When it was cleaned up, she would keep it that way. About his person, Alton was always in a freshly laundered shirt and otherwise had a well-scrubbed look that she loved.

Their next date was a disappointment. Alton never showed up. She was embarrassed but told her friends there must have been some misunderstanding.

When she mentioned it to Alton, he shrugged. "I don't want to see those asinine people on every date. Let's go to the house. I want to show you what they've done."

A ring of fear enveloped Lila. "Alton, those are my friends. How am I to deal with your hateful remark?"

Alton frowned. "I'm sorry. That was stupid thing to say. I just like it when we're together, alone."

The house was spotless. The papers and the journals were now in neat piles. Lila shook off her anger at Alton. "You did good," she said.

"So," he said, "can we get married now?"

Lila laughed lightly at him. "Too soon," she said, shaking her head but smiling at him. In her own bed that night, Lila's thoughts took flight. Her prestige as Alton's wife would give her entry into a whole new world. She might be invited to join the research team charting early childhood cognitive abilities. And if Alton was all that people said of him, she would be center stage in a whole intellectual world beyond her dreams. She could see herself as the gracious hostess for Alton when he met with international scientists. She imagined how she would smile modestly when he was praised.

She hadn't realized how grasping she had become. Was her need for respect from others warping her judgment? What are the realities? she asked herself. He's thirteen years older. So? He has no family. Well, she only had her brother and ailing father. The pluses? She loved music, mainly bluegrass, but also classical. Her mother always had the classical station on when she busied herself around the house. She attended dance recitals and athletic events. He loved classical music; he liked to bike and walk. They both desired a simple life. The essentials, of course, but she also admired beautiful things, not necessarily to own them, but she responded to a fine painting, to art glass, to a handsome piece of furniture. *Idea*. She'd ask him to go with her to the U art gallery and gauge his reactions. More important than all that, would he care about *her* thoughts? Would he be a listener? She had reservations. She decided to pose a searching question at their next meeting.

The next day, sitting in the living room of his house, she asked him what he wished he would be doing five years from now. He thought for a moment.

"If I can just get past a problem I'm having with my calculations, it's very complicated, but if I can take the next step I will be on my way to proving what is as yet conjecture on my part. By then, I will have proof and can share it with the world," he nodded as if convincing himself.

Lila smiled. "That's a noble wish," Lila responded, smiling at her unintended pun. "Would you like to hear my wishes five years from now?"

"Yes," said Alton.

"Well, I'd like to have my master's and work on a study of young children's learning patterns. I think by then I'd like to have one or maybe even two children."

"At school?" Alton said quizzically.

"No," Lila laughed. "My own children, Alton."

"Yes, of course," he said, taking her hand.

Then he bent and kissed her. She responded to him, wanting more. That drove her on. As long as the attraction was there, perhaps that's what marriage really was—a trade-off of pluses for minuses. It was time to move on in her life.

The next day at the art gallery, they cruised past one abstract painting to another until they came upon a room where paintings from the Hudson River School filled the walls. These Alton scrutinized carefully—the long views of mountains and valleys in sunlight and mist made him smile and take her hand. "I'd like to find that place and stand right there on the spot Palmer painted," he said. She squeezed his hand in hers.

Yes, she thought, she'd welcomed the adventure that would be marriage to this complex man. She held her breath, would he ask her again? That evening he asked her if she was ready to give him an answer. She said yes to Alton Ostro.

Suddenly, she was wildly happy. She had made a decision. She felt empowered. She wanted everyone she cared about to celebrate their decision. Winter break was approaching. She asked Alton if she could put up a Christmas tree in his living room and throw a party. He agreed and pressed on her a sum of money for the occasion.

Lila finally had her chance to experience some of the frills of the holiday season. She invited Judith and her family to the party, insisting that they bring a Hanukkah menorah and light their candles. Dr. Mayfield and his wife agreed to join them but only for a short while as they had several other commitments during the festive season. Vera Sternberg, the principal, glided in, wearing a long Indian gown. Clive, Alton's graduate assistant, came with his girlfriend. Lila invited Frederic and several colleagues who brought their children. Lila laid out floor games that they could play and later take home.

Lila put all the dishes through the dishwasher in preparation for the evening. They had never been used by Alton. She scrubbed the pots. She made a large pan of lasagna and a huge green salad. Judith brought the batter for potato pancakes and oil that she fried on Alton's kitchen stove. "They have to be hot and fresh," she declared, draining them on paper towels and then placing them on a platter with a sauce boat of applesauce. Frederic brought a vegetarian dish of his own devising, stocked with slabs of zucchini, purple eggplant, and red and yellow peppers, sprinkled with oregano and other spices. There was wine and cheese. The conversation was lively, and everyone, including Alton, ate heartily. He even commented on the potato pancakes to Judith's pleasure.

She warmed to Judith's children lighting each candle in the Hanukkiah on what, it turned out, was the final day of the festival. Vera Sternberg stood by as the lights were kindled, joining Judith in the blessing over the candles. Ceremony had a certain solace all its own for Lila.

Vera looked on with concern. She had been in Alton Ostro's company a few years ago. They had met at a dinner party, and being single, she had spoken to him after the dinner about getting together. "Sure," he said. But he never called. She invited him to her home for a gathering. Then she explained that the other couple had an emergency and couldn't come. She wanted to get to know him.

She was a passionate person, and it had been some time. She found him cold, withdrawn, and nasty in a way. He had nothing to say about her elaborate dinner she had fussed over and that he gobbled down. He sat across from her, listening with a slight smirk while she attempted to draw him out. She wanted to warn Lila about Ostro, that he was an unpleasant creature. But now, at this gathering, she saw Lila so happy and Ostro acting actually human; she began to doubt her instincts. Better say nothing. Perhaps, after all, it was her that he disliked. Perhaps Lila could bring him out, mold that piece of clay into human form. With that thought in mind, she withdrew, thanking her hostess and nodding to Ostro.

This was so nice, Lila thought. This is what married life can be. She was deeply pleased with herself and Alton.

When it came time to toss out the drying tree, she laughed at herself. She simply had to have that experience.

Chapter 9

They planned the wedding for late May, after the school year ended. Lila invited her father and his wife, but they begged off. Her dad had to use oxygen off and on, and flying was problematic for him. Her brother Martin would come with his little son to help his wife cope with one less child while he was away. Judith would be her maid of honor, and Clive, Alton's assistant, would stand up for him. They'd be married in the college chapel in a civil ceremony conducted by Dr. Mayfield.

Her father sent her the complete silver service that her mother had patiently purchased, one five-piece setting at a time, until she had all twelve settings. Grace had laughed in her last months that although her silver chest was finally complete, she had no strength left to have a dinner for twelve. Opening the chest, Lila's eyes welled up with tears. She saw her mother, in her mind's eye, so weak and spent. She wanted to hold her, but all she could do was kiss her fingertips and pass her hand over the chest's wooden cover.

Lila was very emotional in the days before the wedding. It was after all, a complete lifestyle change. She looked forward to marriage as a cocoon of love and affection. Alton was not a warm person, she had to admit. Although she took heart that he had been very attentive in the weeks before the wedding, moving her books and records to his house and filling her car with clothes and sundries that they had brought upstairs to the closets.

Judith was supportive, assuring her that everyone has last-minute nerves. She surprised Lila by giving her a gift of a silver *hamsa,* a hand-shaped amulet that Jews and other peoples from the Middle East believed would ward off evil spirits and bring good luck. It had a vivid turquoise stone in the middle and hung from a silver chain. Judith said the hand-shaped pendant would protect her. Lila had little jewelry, so she was thrilled and begged Judith to put the pretty *hamsa* around her neck.

"What a lovely gift, Judy. I shall wear it always, and I hope it will protect me," she laughed knowingly at Judith who had voiced her concerns about Alton. Lila and Judith smiled together in the mirror at her pendant and each other. Her spirits lifted when she touched the silver charm.

Her brother Martin and six-year-old Brett flew in the night before the wedding. Lila made a makeshift dinner at Alton's house. She apologized for her groom being absent; Alton had his monthly seminar, but she hoped he would be home before they left for their motel. Little Brett was a lively child, thrilled to be on a trip with his father. He helped Lila unwrap the presents she had received. Frederic gave her a gourmet cookbook, and the women she taught with had gotten together and bought a microwave oven for the couple. There were few modern appliances in the house, and Lila was delighted with the gift. Brett was sitting on the couch half-asleep, and Martin said they'd have to go. Soon after they left, Alton, on his bicycle, returned home.

Lila and Alton selected simple gold rings to exchange at the wedding. There had been no engagement ring. For the wedding, Lila wore the white suit that she could use all summer. She walked in, escorted by her brother. Her jacket was low-cut and on her blouse, the *hamsa*'s bright turquoise eye surveyed the crowd. Holding the bouquet Judith had brought her, she approached the altar smiling. Alton stood there pale and solemn. Her fellow teachers and several members of Alton's department filled the first few rows of the chapel, looking on with varied expressions. Dean Mayfield pronounced the time-honored words. Her nephew presented the two rings on a pillow without dropping them. He did his job so well. Lila bent to kiss him. "You're pretty," he said, smiling at her. Alton kissed her next, on the cheek.

In an adjoining room of the chapel, Frederic had orchestrated a brief reception of champagne and a cake he had created with orange-flavored layers wrapped in whipped cream. The cake was delicious, and Lila, whispering in his ear, congratulated him on his steps to becoming a chef.

"Who will I dine with now?" he said plaintively. Alton's colleagues and her fellow teachers toasted the couple, demolished the cake, finished the champagne, and the wedding was over.

Martin had a camera; he asked the bride and groom to pose for a picture. Lila smiled at the camera, but Alton abruptly turned around. "No pictures," he said bluntly. Then, thinking better of it, he added, "Take the others, no problem."

Dr. Mayfield said he had made reservations at a hotel restaurant for the bridal party, and off they went. If it weren't for Harvey's gaiety, it would have been a solemn occasion. Alton had little to say, and Martin looked concerned, but Lila and Judith and little Brett laughed at Harvey's buffoonery.

When the maitre d' came over with the check, he seemed uncertain as to whom to give it to. "Do you have a credit card?" Lila whispered to Alton. He shook his head.

"I don't think I have enough cash." Martin signaled the waiter for the check, with a sigh.

Outside, waiting for their cars, Martin took Lila aside. "I don't know, sis, this guy doesn't seem to be with it. And how old is he, for god's sake?"

"Thank you for taking the check, Martin, that was sweet of you. We were dopey not to have anticipated the dinner. Can I pay you back?"

"Don't be silly. It's fine. It's the least I could do for my little sister."

"Listen, Martin, I know what I'm getting into. Alton needs a lot of work, but I think he's worth it. He might win a Nobel one day! You'll see. It was good of you to come, and Brett is such a pleasure. Things are working out for you at home. I'm so glad."

They kissed good-bye; Martin was off to the airport, the other guests to their homes, and Alton and Lila to theirs.

Chapter 10

Since Alton refused to own a credit card, she had to ask him for cash each week. They settled on an allowance for her to run the household, stopping at the bank to make a substantial withdrawal.

During the summer, Lila took a course for her master's and also supervised a play group for pre-K kids at the local public school. She offered to share her salary for household expenses, but Alton told her to save her money for herself. If she needed a new blouse or personal item, she paid for it herself. If she wanted to buy him new shirts to replace his frayed ones, she had to ask him to withdraw the cash so she could shop. He never refused to do so.

He had recently won the Persley Prize for innovative thinking, a sum he shared with his department. Rent for the house and utilities came out of his bank account where his salary was deposited. In time, she hoped to prove to him she wasn't a spendthrift and he could trust her with charge cards, but she didn't want to do anything behind his back; that was no way to start married life.

She was pleased to see that he was a neat person and liked things orderly. Only the second bedroom, which he called his office, was off-limits to her cleaning passion. He allowed her to dust and vacuum but not to touch his papers.

She wasn't surprised that he was not much of a lover. Perhaps, she reasoned, that's why he put off intimacies until they were married. Now what she had hoped would be extended loving foreplay was limited to three thrusts and he was done, rolling over and snoring. He seemed shy to be naked in front of her.

She decided to take a bold step with her reticent mate. On the second Sunday after the wedding, seeing him in the shower, she ducked behind the shower curtain and squeezed inside with him. He was surprised, but when she started to soap him, he caught on and soaped her in return. They both laughed, and then he gasped, pushing her out of the shower. He cowered in the corner. She turned off the water and handed him a towel. He staggered to their bedroom.

"Alton, are you okay?"

"Yes, yes," he grunted, closing the door. She showered again and dried off. When she peeked inside, he was asleep. The incident was not mentioned.

A week later, she woke to sounds in the bathroom. Alton was showering. It was 3:00 a.m.

"Alton, what are you doing?" she called to him.

"I have to go to the lab to run some figures." She protested the hour, but he said he had to do this while it was fresh in his mind. He'd see her later.

His hours were erratic. They'd agree on a time for dinner; he wouldn't appear. She offered to pick him up one evening when it rained and waited in her little car for him to exit the physics building at the time arranged. After a half hour, she drove home. He didn't return until morning for a shower and change of clothes. He had slept in the lab. She went off to work, more than a little annoyed.

I have to remember he's special, she told herself driving along to the school on the education campus. I have a duty to nurture him. I have to take care of Alton. Something in his past must have traumatized him. I can't say he's selfish, but he seems to have no idea of another's feelings. Or am I being silly? He may be so wrapped up in his unified theory, and I don't know what—that he can't separate. Maybe if we had a child, he'd become more invested in those around him. She realized that they had only indirectly talked about having children, but she longed to have a child.

When she asked him one night, he shrugged, "If you want," he said. She stopped taking the pill. In three months, she was pregnant, not that Alton noticed.

She learned to eat at six, as had been her usual time, and not wait for him. When they had concert tickets, however, Alton managed to be prompt. He never wanted to socialize in the lobby during intermission, reading the program instead or closing his eyes and meditating on what he had heard. Lila looked at him one night, with his hands on his knees and eyes shut. She thought with chagrin, He loves music, but as for people, I think he's tone-deaf.

"I'll take a break," she whispered in his ear, going to the lobby and visiting with their next-door neighbors, the Bradys, a retired couple, before returning to her seat. It was a mild night in November; they had taken a brisk walk to the university theater. On the way home, Lila told her husband she was pregnant. "Good," he said, "do I have to do anything special?"

"You did your part," she said lightly, smiling. "But I do want to prepare the other bedroom for the baby."

"You can't do that. I have my papers in there and my books and records where there is no room at my lab."

"I went up to the third floor, Alton. We could make that attic space into a terrific library. I have files and books too. I could have my things in one part, you the rest."

"So, if it's so terrific, put the baby up there and leave my papers alone."

"Alton," Lila said sharply. "I don't believe you. You're putting books and papers ahead of a child's welfare!"

"Yes, I am. I can't be disturbed. You knew that. This marriage thing is a little too much for me. I thought I could live as I had."

"Perhaps you'd like me to disappear, Alton."

"I don't know. I'll give it more time."

"Thanks a bunch. And by the way, the grass needs cutting."

"Now you're unreal," he said. Lila began to laugh. If she didn't, she would cry. She walked ahead of him to the house, but he managed to scoot around her and opened the door with his key. They went to bed without speaking. In the morning, she woke to a clatter in the yard. Alton was cutting the grass.

"I have my seminar with the graduate students at four o'clock," he told her when he came in for breakfast. "It could go on until late and then some of us may go out for food. Don't wait supper for me."

"Thanks for telling me. I'll have dinner with Judith. Harvey is out buying a car, so I'll keep her company." They parted amicably. She held her face up for a kiss; he pecked her on the cheek. She was reading in bed that night when she heard the door slam. Alton was cursing and shouting.

"What is it?" Lila yelled at the head of the stairs, frightened.

Alton looked up, fury in his face, his lower jaw protruding, his teeth clenched. Lila drew back. He banged his fist on the foyer table.

"Damn him! Damn him, the rotten fool!"

Now that she knew she was not involved, Lila came down the stairs. "Alton, what happened, dear?"

"The blasted seminar! Last month I gave the fools a problem I was having and asked them to study the matter for the next session. This cretin came up with a formula that totally contradicted my calculations! He's a lunatic! He pointed to a gap in my figures. He completely misunderstood the math. He's the one with the mistake. It may look good, but there's an error in his calcs. I know it. I just know it! Now I have to take the time to disprove his figures." He slapped his hand down again, this time on the stairway railing.

Lila took his arm. "Come have tea. If you prove him wrong, it'll only strengthen your theory, dear."

"My theory, as you call it," he shot back, "is airtight. It doesn't need strengthening! I don't mind being shown the way to the next step, but this, this just slows me down, puts me back. I'll have to run his miserable calculations for days to find the error." He groaned, "You don't understand." He sat at the kitchen table with his head in his hands.

Lila wondered how he handled the situation. "What did you tell the student?" she asked softly.

"What did I tell him? What could I tell him? That he did a good deal of work and I would look it over after class. We went on to something else. I didn't go out with the students. I went to my office and looked at his figures. My head was spinning. The calculations look good—but they're not, I assure you. Damn him. Damn again."

"Please, Alton, you did exactly the right thing praising the student for the work he did. That was fine. You haven't eaten, have something then. I'll warm some soup? An omelet? Anything?"

"All right, an omelet and this tea." He ate in silence.

Lila quietly broached an idea she had been thinking about that might help Alton. TM, transcendental meditation.

"Alton," she said quietly. "So many people find meditation very helpful in relieving the stress we all feel. There's a speaker at the Student Union on Wednesday. I'd like to go, will you join me?"

"I know all about that," he said without looking up. "Music is my meditation. And right now, that would be no help either. I'm in a real quagmire here, Lila."

"Ah," she said, in a sympathetic voice.

She heard him pacing in the guest room, off and on all night. His hours at the lab were his own. He could sleep as late as he wanted. She had to be up early for her four-year-olds at school. She tossed in bed alone, wondering if she had been any help to him. At least he had calmed down. It must be horrible to feel your work has been faulty, and he puts so much psychic energy into it. It would be devastating to have his figures disproved. She felt for him. At the same time, she realized her limitations. His needs go way beyond a devoted wife. If only I could get him into some therapy, she thought. But how?

She tried to put Alton's hysteria out of her mind. I have to keep myself healthy. I have to think of my baby now, she told herself. The thought of the child, growing in her womb, changed her mood. Smiling, she fell asleep.

The dispute about the spare room was resolved. Alton would keep his cherished room and sleep in the single bed in there. She would have the baby in their bedroom. If he wanted to visit, well, he'd have to ask, or else move his library upstairs. That time was five months off. They'd worry about the details later.

Judith called her up a few days later when Lila had returned home from school.

"Can you imagine what that crazy husband of mine did?"

"No-o-o," said Lila, surprised that Judith had anything but praise for Harvey, at the same time kind of pleased.

"He bought a motorcycle!"

"I thought he was buying a car," Lila said bemused.

"I told him he was going through a midlife crisis. Can you imagine? And if he ever tries to give one of the children a ride, I'll murder him."

"Didn't you say you needed a station wagon," Lila rejoined. Judith had had another boy, and the assumption was that they would be chauffeuring Nathan's soccer pals around in a few years.

"I'm to have the big car. He just needs the bike to tool around on and to go to work. 'What do we need another car for?' he tells me."

Lila wondered if she should share her debacle with Alton, to show she wasn't the only one with a recalcitrant husband. Don't muddy the waters and gossip about her marriage, she decided. There was peace between her and Alton for the moment.

She was afraid to arouse his anger by asking him how his quest to find his student's error came out. One night at dinner, he commented, "You never asked me about my calculations and the student," he charged.

"I thought it best to wait for you to tell me, dear."

"I found his error, at the same time, I saw why my presentation may have led him astray, and I fine-tuned the figures. I plan to explain this to the seminar next week."

"I think that is wonderful. It is a teaching moment, as they say, to see that the professor himself can have such a productive conversation with the students. I'm sure the grad students will respect you even further for it."

"Well, yes," he said, returning to his plate and spearing a forkful. "It's nice of you to say that." A second later, he slammed his hand on the table, rattling the dishes. "Damn him nevertheless. I wasted precious time. Does he realize that? He smirked when I gave him the corrections in my lab. I'd like to throttle the guy! I'm the one that has to approve his dissertation. Let him sweat!" Alton's jaw was out. His anger frightened her.

Sadness enveloped Lila. Alton was not only manic, her husband was mean! What should she do? What could she do? Hope that this was just an incident? The graduate student did sound like a nasty stumbling block. Maybe the debacle with him would pass.

Chapter 11

The Baby Is Born

Lila continued teaching while pregnant. She was assigned two teachers in training. The demonstration school existed to train education majors in the college, as well as for research. Two college seniors had been observing her class part of each day; now they were ready to work with groups of students. Later in the semester, Lila asked the student teachers to take turns conducting a lesson or leading an activity of their own devising. She sat on a chair in the back of the room to observe and later discuss with the student how it went. Both girls were bright and cheerful.

Estralita worried her, however, because she was very overweight. The kids responded to her willingly, but the boys giggled that she was "a fatty." Estralita was near tears overhearing them one day and asked Lila what to do.

"We have to put less emphasis on how people look and dress with the kids," Lila said. "You are the best example because you are kind and caring, and that's what makes a person beautiful. This will be an ongoing thing for you, so think about how you best can defuse these remarks.

Meanwhile, you are doing a good job, and when the kids respond to your lessons, they forget about anything else."

When Estralita left to attend her regular senior classes, Lila made a point with the children that people are different in size, in shape, and the color of their hair and skin. "The things to look for are helpfulness, kindness, what's inside a person." Lila patted her chest and asked the students to do the same. What's Inside became the class motto.

But now Lila was in her seventh month and she spoke to Vera Steinberg about taking leave, and her replacement.

"Good," said the principal warmly. "I have someone in the wings. You don't know Maxine. She has been on maternity leave and is now ready to come back to the classroom. Please come to the conference room to meet her next week and have her meet the students. I'm thrilled for you, by the way. Things are going well, I hope."

"Just fine," Lila cooed, wishing it were so. The following week, she introduced her class to Maxine, who would take over. She promised to bring the baby into class to show them, but by May the school would be out for the summer vacation, so they would not meet the infant after all.

———

"I am going to buy things for the baby," Lila said one morning at breakfast when she was on home.

"Yes, what do you need?" Alton asked casually.

"The usual; a crib, a dressing table, a carriage, and clothes to bring the baby home in. Judith wants to give me a baby shower, but I told her no."

"What the devil is a baby shower?"

"Oh, Alton, never mind. But this bothers me: When my time comes, I'll need you to drive me to the hospital. You do have a driver's license?" Alton nodded while spooning his oatmeal.

"Well, I think you should drive my car around so that you are used to it, don't you agree, Daddy-to-be?"

"I suppose." He went to his stash in the guest room and doled out the money she would need.

She and Judith went off to the baby store, laughing gaily at the thought that they would be mothers together.

"I have some of Noah's baby clothes to give you, but being you're having a girl, I guess you'll want pink blankets and stuff."

"I'll take whatever you have, honey," Lila said. "I don't like to press Alton too much."

"How's he taking the baby coming?"

Lila sighed. "I made him feel my tummy when she kicked. I thought he'd be thrilled. He just said 'Hah,' whatever that means."

"He's a tough nut, Lila."

"Yes, I can't deny I'm disappointed. But I'm working on him. He's my project now that I'm on maternity leave from school."

Lila had the choice of keeping her maiden name at the school, but she had become Mrs. Ostro there. It was hubris, she realized later. Nothing but damned pride, she told herself. Vera Steinberg, the principal, relayed that she had a mother ask, "Ostro, is she related to Alton Ostro?"

"And when I said yes, that you were his wife, she was most impressed." Lila grinned, and the two of them laughed lightly.

As her time drew near, Lila asked Alton to drive her to the hospital grounds, a practice run for him. He drove flawlessly. She smiled at him, grateful for his competence.

"Now that we've got that under control, Alton, dear, please sleep home at night. You never know when the baby may decide to emerge."

"I'll do what I can," he said, clipping his words.

"Alton, you can't put yourself first when the baby is concerned. You have to make adjustments."

When the obstetrician told her that she was dilated and the baby might come in the next thirty-six hours, she called Alton at the lab and said he should be sure to be available.

The crib and carriage arrived from the baby store. Her neighbor, Mrs. Brady came down from her porch to watch. She called to Lila. "I'm so excited. It's like when my Luke was born. Now, Lila, you call on me anytime. I won't be a pest, but I'd love to help you."

Lila waved as she went to the house with the delivery men to make certain they would set up the crib. She called Ella Brady on the phone.

"You know, I am sure I will need your advice. There are no grandmas on the scene, I'm afraid."

"Anytime," Ella Brady repeated.

When her contractions started, Alton was nowhere to be found. She timed them; they were getting close. She could not fool around. She called Ella Brady.

"I'm asking your help sooner that we thought, Ella. Could you drive me to the hospital? I think the baby's coming."

Alvin Brady, zipping up his jacket, was ready first. He brought the car into the Ostros' driveway. "Come along now," he said at the door. Ella Brady took the back seat. As they drove slowly to the hospital, Lila was twisting in pain, trying not to make a sound. Alvin was a cautious driver. Lila hoped they would make it in time. When the intake nurse saw Lila bent over, she put her in a wheelchair and spirited her away.

"Go home, it's getting dark," Lila called to the elderly Bradys. "Alton will be coming along in a minute."

She had an easy delivery and woke to find tiny little Chloe in a bassinette near her bed. She called Judith. "I've had the baby, Judy. Come and see."

Judith arrived, carrying a bunch of pink roses in a vase, oohing and ahhing at Chloe. She insisted on tracking down Alton for Lila.

She kept her thoughts to herself, but Lila could see her friend was steaming. She covered the phone. "The secretary told me he's at his seminar and was not to be disturbed."

"Tell him he's a father when you see him, okay?" Lila heard her say. Judith carefully put down the phone in its cradle. "She said that the seminar had just begun and it would be a couple of hours, but congratulations."

"Don't be too hard on Alton," Lila whispered. "He's having a difficult time with this. But I have my baby, that's the important thing. And I picked her name myself. He couldn't care less about such things."

"All the same, I have to say it, Lila, he's a shit! I'm sorry, Lila. I shouldn't have said that."

Lila held back tears; she was too proud to let Judith see how hurt she was by Alton's mindless neglect. She had looked forward to his kiss when he entered the room and joy light his solemn face upon seeing his child. He didn't appear that night. After Judith left and before she fell asleep, Lila tried not to weep, but then she thought-- just let it out. She turned over a pillow wet with her tears.

Ella Brady was a constant companion when she and Chloe came home. She helped Lila start to nurse the baby, encouraging both mother and the child, who refused the breast at first. But when Chloe caught on, Lila was ecstatic.

"She's got it, she's got it," she called to Ella. Her neighbor smiled in shared joy and asked how the new father was doing. Lila laughed to herself. When he saw the child in the hospital, he said "Very nice, nice baby," like he was looking over a car in the showroom. She put the baby in his arms, hoping for a smile. "Hello," he said to the child, looking surprised that she didn't answer and handing the baby back to Lila.

"The father is doing as well as can be expected," Lila said. Actually, he was making Lila nervous.

The week before the baby was born, he had moved into the guest room. She had taken up the many magazines and scientific periodicals she found strewn on the floor there and, organizing them by date, shelved them in the bookcase in the room. It made sense to her, but Alton was grumbling.

"How am I to find what I want in here?"

"Well, dear," she had said patiently, "if you know the date—"

"I rely on the covers to find what I decide to read—not—on—the—date! That's why I like them spread out." And he began tossing the magazines on the floor.

Lila closed the door to the guest room and hauled her ungainly body into a chair downstairs. He was a most disagreeable man, she admitted to herself. What exactly was she getting out of this marriage? Sexually, he was totally missing as a lover. When she attempted to caress his lean body, he moved her hands aside. He performed his one-two-three routine, then rolled over away from her. She pressed against him trying to reach some satisfaction herself, but he shied away. I made a devil's bargain, she decided. I romanticized helping him create whatever it is he's searching for, of being the nurturing wife of an admittedly difficult man, a walking brain. But he is really cruel, she sighed to herself. Then the little person inside her kicked. Lila laughed. "You agree with me, baby. We'll have each other, that'll make it all right."

Chapter 12

Little Chloe slept in her crib in what had been the room Lila shared with Alton. She nursed her whenever she cried. It was lovely. After being up several times during the night, she slept through Alton's breakfast time. She apologized in the evening when he came home. He shrugged, "I had coffee at the commons as I used to before."

The day she took the baby for her checkup, she didn't have dinner ready when he came home.

"I'm trying to cooperate with you, Lila," he said. "I'm home on time, so what's the problem?"

"You might want to know how Chloe's checkup went, Alton."

"Yes?"

"She's ten pounds already and has begun sleeping almost six hours."

"Okay, so let's have dinner. I'll get the wine. We'll drink to the ten-pound baby."

Lila could have slapped his face at this ridiculous remark but she held herself back. A glass of wine would be good.

One night, the baby was fretful; nothing could quiet her. Suddenly, Alton burst into the room.

"Can't you get her to shut up?" he yelled.

"I don't know what's wrong. Maybe it's her tummy. I'm rocking her, but she doesn't stop. Here, you try," was her sudden inspiration.

"Not me, not me," he said with fear in his eyes. He retreated to his room.

Lila finally succeeded in getting a monumental burp out of Chloe, and then she settled down.

Another night, Alton was so irritated by Chloe's crying that he shouted, "Get that kid to shut up!"

"Alton," Lila said, trying to keep her voice even, "*you* shut up. How dare you yell at us in the middle of night! Just go to your room and leave us alone."

In no mood to argue further and totally on edge, she needed some air. Lila bundled up the baby, put her in the carriage in the downstairs hall and went outside to the porch. The rocking of the carriage always calmed the little one. She wheeled it slowly, back and forth. A light went on next door. She saw Mr. Brady in the window, looking down at her in his pajamas. He turned away, shaking his head.

In early June, with school out and Chloe's first birthday approaching, her fellow teachers came to visit, bringing along their own small children to celebrate. Chloe was trying to walk, holding on, falling down, tumbling over. The other children were captivated by her antics.

Then old grumpy appeared. He nodded to the women but took Lila aside.

"Those kids could have diseases, get them out of here."

"Alton, my friends wouldn't bring kids here that are sick. Be nice, we're celebrating Chloe's birthday. Have some cake. Give her a hug."

"Later," he said, going up the stairs.

She would have to have a heart-to-heart talk with Alton. After a glass of wine at dinner, that seemed to relax him, and she felt loosened up too. She began, "Alton, Chloe is your child, yet you seem so remote with her. And it's her birthday."

"Aren't I providing?"

"Yes, you are, and very well. I was just wondering if something in your childhood had made you fearful of relating to our child. Can you think of anything? Was your mother—"

"Don't ever speak about my mother!" Alton paled. He was silent, but his eyes burned with fury. Then he said in a wounded voice, "I've never been around such a little child is all. And I'm under a lot of pressure in my work."

"I do understand. I think, though, if you could let go of it a little bit when you come home, you might feel refreshed when you go back to work. You know, they say a break gives you new energy."

"I'm not a factory worker. I don't need a break. While we're talking, I really wish you and the child could go somewhere until she grows up a little and doesn't do that babbling when we're trying to eat."

"Go away? You mean for a couple of years?"

"That would be all right. Yes. Or you could board her somewhere. I liked it before."

"Chloe and I could go away permanently, if you wish. We could get divorced."

"Who said anything about that!" Alton was shouting. He got up from his chair and looked down at Lila with hate in his eyes. "I'd kill you first!"

The outburst seemed to steady him. "I didn't mean that," he mouthed through tight lips. "It's just that it was nice before," his voice trailed off.

That night, Lila felt the presence of someone in the room. It was Alton. He was looking down at the sleeping babe in her crib. Lila watched carefully. What was he doing? Admiring the child, or something terrifyingly worse?

"Alton, can I help you?" she asked, trying to keep her voice level.

"You could stay, if the child could go," he said pleasantly. Lila froze. Alton abruptly turned. She saw he was holding a pillow at his chest. Then he was gone. Lila leaped from bed and peered into the crib. Chloe was sleeping, breathing in and out with a slight smile crossing her lips for a moment.

Too stunned to think, she paused there a minute. Should she scream at him and tell him he was crazy and needed help? Should she call the police? Go to the dean? She was trembling with frustration. She tried to breathe deeply to calm herself. Her marriage had been a huge mistake. She tried to think rationally. She would deliver an ultimatum to Alton then and there! She opened the door to Alton's room. He was standing at the window.

"Alton, turn around and face me," Lila said firmly. "Tomorrow I'm calling the psychiatrist at the clinic. You will go to see him. You need help, Alton. I cannot stay here with you if you do not get help. Is that clear?"

"Never," he called, turning his back on her. "Never! Go away."

Protecting her daughter was now her only thought. She was afraid to live in his house a minute longer. How could she ever rest with him next door? He asked her to disappear. She would disappear. Lila was never so sure of anything in her life as she was that night. Gently she lifted Chloe from her crib and placed her in the bed. She would try to sleep, one hand on the baby's blanket.

The next morning, she withdrew her money from the bank in cash. She stowed it in a six-pack cooler bag. She did the laundry, gave Chloe lunch, and put her down for her nap.

It was essential that she leave before Alton might return at six. She gathered her vital papers and placed them in a manila envelope. She mentally called off a list of basics as she assembled her needs: Clothes for Chloe, and diapers, and juice packs and some baby food, and a spoon and bibs, she told herself as she raced around the house. She had a small duffel in which she stuffed Chloe's things. For herself, she dug out the duffel she had used at college and added slacks, a sweater, a jacket for herself, toiletries, and the bag that she filled with the cash. It was getting toward five thirty. She had wanted to give Chloe dinner, but there was no time. The phone rang. Lila held her breath. It was Clive, Alton's graduate assistant.

"Dr. Ostro told me to call, Mrs. Ostro."

"Yes?" she said.

"He asked me to tell you he won't be home 'til late. Not to wait dinner for him."

Letting out her breath, Lila said a weak "Thank you, Clive," and hung up. Good, now I have more time. Lila realized Chloe could have dinner. Chloe had been chattering to herself in her playpen while Lila packed their things.

"Come baby, chop, chop. Here's a nice veggie plate for you, and then we'll take a long ride in the car." Chloe grinned at her. "Car," she said. Chloe liked to ride and look out the window. It'll be dark, Lila thought. She'll sleep most of the way.

Wearing a warm-up suit, a sweater, and sneakers, Lila started the trip by filling her tank at the gas station. Her car was an '85, no airbag, but it ran well and the tires were new—her father had insisted on that a month ago when she read him her mileage. She traveled local roads until she could join the highway, then she barreled on. It was 9:30 by then, and she realized she had been too preoccupied to bother eating all day. Now she was starving

Lila pulled into a rest stop with Chloe on her hip; she went inside and ordered a cheese sandwich and a bowl of soup. The radio in the café was playing Kenny Rogers's gambling song—"Know when to fold 'em, know when to walk away and know when to run." Lila let out a low groan. Yes, Kenny, she thought, I gambled, I lost, I was trying not to fold, but then I knew I had to run. She sighed. Confirming her decision made her feel more relaxed. She smiled at Chloe enjoying her sippy cup. The child was wide awake after napping in the car. Lila knew she should stop for the night, but she was fleeing from Alton, and the further she was from him, the safer she felt. Her energy level was at its peak. She could never have closed her eyes in a motel. Keep going, she thought. She hoped to reach her brother early the next afternoon. She paid her bill and left for Pennsylvania in the little green car.

Chapter 13

Alton

In a sense, Alton had always been alone. He had hardly known his father who died when he was a baby. His mother's attentions were so erratic that her parents insisted that the child live with them. His mother came along with him at first. He remembers looking into her eyes with their wide pupils, while she spoke to him in baby talk. Only later did he realize she must have been on drugs. All he knew was that her parents argued with her every night and ended screaming at her. One day, when he came home from school, he found a note on his pillow. "Be a good boy, Allie, and mind your grandparents. Kisses from Mom."

What does it mean, he asked his grandmother, Kate.

"Your mother is gone for good, and that means you are our charge from now on. We'll do everything to make you happy, Alton," his grandmother said. "Try not to miss her."

Alton was puzzled. He didn't have any feeling for his mother. How could he miss her? His interests were reading *Scientific America* and *National Geographic*. He greedily grasped at the work in his classes, reading beyond the lessons. He performed so well in science and math that he was skipped to ninth grade when he was twelve. His classmates were two years older; they didn't bother with him. He came home from school, did his homework, and read his magazines.

His grandfather asked to have a talk with him one evening. He wondered if Alton would like to speak about the changes he was going through.

"You're entering your teen years. Your voice is deep now, and you're tall and strong. If you have questions about anything, I'm here to help answer them."

"I don't have questions. I'm fine," Alton said quietly.

"I want you to have another interest besides your books, my boy," his grandfather continued. "You're home alone too much. I want to sign you up for the tennis clinic at the Y. You'll be good at it, Alton."

So Alton went to tennis clinic twice a week, and he proved an apt student, putting low forehand shots over the net, sprinting for short balls, tipping them back to score a point. The coach saw his potential and spent time with him after class concentrating on Alton's serve. It had the speed, he was told; he just needed to work on its accuracy. Once he nailed it down, the coach moved Alton into the junior players' Saturday game.

Alton felt good running and hitting the ball; it was invigorating to keep moving. But he got no particular pleasure in winning a game. It was just a matter of sending the ball back until the other player missed. No big deal. He practiced as the coach directed, and he kept improving.

His grandfather, who was an avid football fan and sports enthusiast, was thrilled with Alton's progress. After a year at the clinic, the coach offered to enter Alton, two other boys, and one girl in the Junior United States Tennis Association competition. His grandfather gave his permission and arranged with the father of another player to bring Alton to the competition.

Lots of parents were in the stands, hugging their kids whether they won or lost. Alton had no one there; his grandfather could not leave work to attend. The father of the teammate he went with took them both out for pizza after the matches were over. He looked at the boy and his father laughing and joking together, and he felt a pain inside that made him angry. Alton's grandfather congratulated him on his win, but the pain persisted.

Alton's strong serve was able to demolish his opponents in his fourteen-and-under age group, but when he was moved up to the next level at fifteen, the coach gave him and one other boy a lecture in strategy.

"You're playing older, more seasoned players now, boys," he said. "Your serve will be answered, Alton. Both you boys will have to use strategy. Get your opponent to one side of the court by sending successive balls toward that corner. Once he is far over, you smash one in the opposite corner. It's not just rallying until one guy misses. It's making him miss. We'll practice that, okay?"

In his first match, Alton got out on the court and tried to move his opponent, but his shots went wild. His serve was answered, so he had to rally to win a point. He won one game in the first set and only one game in the second. He was trounced 6–1. 6–1. He was mortified. He never cared when he won, but he was furious when he lost. "A waste of time," he told himself. The other boy held on. The coach told Alton not to worry. It was only the first of many games to come. Alton shook his head, but he didn't show up on Saturday for practice. His grandfather questioned him.

"I have other interests now," he told him. "I'm going to the science lab on Saturdays. My teacher and I are working on a project."

It was true. His teacher, Mr. Maxwell, always claimed he discovered Alton. When his student was a high school junior he had him taking math and science classes at the junior college in their upstate New York town. The high school department couldn't keep up with him. Alton loved the work. Math was such a relief. You did the work; you got the answer. Physics had its laws that explained the physical world. It was only later in college that he began to question some of those "laws."

Working in the lab with the other high school seniors was a hassle for Alton. He was sixteen to their eighteen. Their notebooks aside, they talked of girls and their conquests in the most vulgar terms. Alton wanted to hold his ears. He spoke up.

"If you want to describe women's reproductive systems, for god's sake, give them the dignity of using the anatomical labels and not this filth. It's hard to hear and disgusting," Alton said heatedly.

"Oh, for sure, Al. Let's be anatomical. I really like Tiffany's vulva," one said.

The others laughed.

"And me, I penetrated the labia minor all the way up to the labia major with Megan," called another. More laughter.

"Rosa has the most inflated mammaries I've ever squeezed," said a third. By this time they were all convulsed by their cleverness. Alton went on with his work, paying the scene no mind. Mr. Maxwell's head could be seen in shadow on the frosted glass door. The sudden silence was a giveaway.

"What's all the hilarity?" the teacher asked, striding in.

"Ostro was giving us a lesson in anatomy, sir," the first prankster said.

Alton looked up from his worktable. He had forgotten the boys in his concentration on the matter he was tackling.

Mr. Maxwell shook his head. They worked silently after that.

He told himself that he didn't care if the others had little regard for him; Mr. Maxwell was his friend. But the salacious talk of his lab mates had aroused him.

A woman was hired to clean on Thursdays while his grandmother was at the hospital where she worked in the gift shop. The woman was there when he came in from school. He usually went to his room after eating a pudding or taking some cheese from the fridge. This day, while he was at the kitchen table, the woman, Serena, said to him, "I am very warm from the vacuuming. Do you mind if I take off my blouse?"

Alton shrugged. What did he care? But then he saw she was naked on top. He had never seen a woman's breasts before, and he stared. He felt a warmth in his thighs looking at her.

"So you are a red-blooded boy after all," she chirped, looking down at him. She approached, holding a meaty breast near his lips. He saw the dark pink nipple rise and, without thinking, put his mouth around it, feeling it with his saliva until he felt a sudden wetness in his trousers. Face aflame, he ran to his room and slammed the door.

Serena knocked and asked him if she could come in. "No!" he shouted. "Go away!"

"It's nothing to be ashamed of," she cooed on the other side of the door.

The next Thursday, he decided not to return home until she was gone. He was in a panic because he wanted to go to her. Almost against his will, he entered the house, hoping she had gone. But she was there, and she revealed more of herself to him and promised she'd show him how to be a man. It became a weekly tussle with him; he didn't want to go home, but he couldn't stop himself. Until the day came when his grandmother returned early and found them on the sofa together. She held her head in grief and growled, "*Get out*, you wretch, I could have you arrested!"

The woman left, but she winked at Alton as she closed the door. Alton was glad it was over.

"Well," said his grandfather later, "you are sowing your wild oats rather early, my boy. That woman went to you, not the other way around. Is that right?" he asked. Alton nodded.

"If you have any questions, shoot. I was a bit of a wild one in my time."

"No, Grandfather, no questions. I'll just forget it."

"There's the lad. Find a nice girl now for yourself." Alton nodded. The subject was closed.

Alton entered the university college before his seventeenth birthday on a full scholarship. He was tall and thin, and his serious demeanor made him seem older than his years. He was awkward socially; he did not fit into the college scene. But as in high school, he didn't care. It was the pursuit of knowledge that gripped him. He loved the university. He looked through a telescope for the first time and marveled at the heavens filled with stars he had never imagined. It was both frightening and wonderful. He toured the mechanical engineering department and saw how hydraulics and gravity were harnessed to make machines work. He loved the physics lab with its well-equipped devices for measurement. There was enough to keep him busy for the four years ahead. The social scene did not concern him.

His roommate, nineteen-year-old Kevin Nealy, was not particularly friendly. One Friday night he said to Alton, "Listen, roomie, tomorrow, stay away between six and ten, okay?"

"Why's that? I had planned some work then."

"Here, take my ticket to the concert. I've got more important things to do than go hear a chamber group play. My girlfriend is coming, and we have plans to be here. *Capiche?*"

Sheepishly, Alton took the ticket. The concert was a revelation. He loved the music. He loved the play of themes that were repeated on different levels from movement to movement. He loved the serenity he felt as the music swelled and faded only to gather force and soar again. He went to the box office at intermission and asked for a concert schedule. From that night on, he never missed one.

He thanked Kevin the next morning.

"Hey," said Kevin, "I'll return the favor anytime."

"Not likely," Alton murmured.

"What, are you gay or something?"

Alton made a face.

"Well, have you ever done it?"

Alton looked at him and nodded grimly. "Too much. I'm off it now."

"That's nuts!" Kevin laughed. "There's never too much."

The next semester, Alton asked and got a room by himself. His pals were fellow nerds at the lab. They did experiments together and took field trips with the professor. Sometimes they ate out together. His lab friends were over twenty-one, and it was supposed that Alton, with his stoic face and quiet demeanor, was too. He acquired a taste for wine on those occasions.

He began a relationship with a girl in the group. She enticed him to participate in sexual activity, but after several sessions, she gave him a book, *The Joy of Sex*, and commanded him to read it. He put it aside and avoided her after that. He had no time to waste on pleasing her.

His grandparents had died—first his grandfather and then his grandmother. He had gone to his grandfather's funeral, but final exams kept him on campus when his grandmother died. He wondered if his mother had come by or if she was still alive. An attorney answered that question for him. He wrote that his grandparents' home had been sold at their request, and this sum, and other monies, had been left to him alone. The money was of no consequence to him. He realized that part of his life as a son and grandson was over. He had no ties. He was just Alton, with no home or person to go to. The university would be his home, he told himself, and that was okay with him.

He stayed on campus through the summers, taking courses and working in the various labs, and he was admitted to graduate study at twenty. From there it was smooth sailing as he mastered every scientific theory and added some hypotheses of his own. At twenty-four, he held a PhD and was appointed an assistant professor with a lab of his own.

He had to teach Physics 101, and that was a challenge. He could expect nothing from his pupils as they didn't seem interested and he was not enchanting them either. He was relieved of teaching chores when his first scientific paper, published in a respected science journal, caused a stir and applause. "The young Dr. Ostro may be on to something quite amazing," read one review. Praises came from other scientific centers, and he was offered a full professorship in a college in California. Alton felt at home where he was and declined the offer. Glowing in the accolades of one of its professors, the administration decided he should be free to pursue his revolutionary ideas without the interruption of teaching chores. The exception was his bimonthly seminars that he had been holding now for fourteen years.

His social life had been limited to invitations from married faculty that needed an extra man at the table. He was a polite guest but generally silent unless the talk was of music or science. He was considered "dry" company. It was Dr. Mayfield who took him in hand.

"You need to get out more," he said. "There are lots of single woman on the faculty. I want you to meet some of them. Find a wife, Alton. It will be good for you."

That night at the reception, Dr. Mayfield pointed to a woman in her thirties, a medical doctor. "She's divorced and very available."

Alton said, "No, not her."

Dr. Mayfield spotted a teacher in the demonstration school. "See the woman listening in that group of women."

Alton gazed at Lila. Her shapely figure and erect posture appealed to him, and when she turned and he saw her face, he said to Mayfield, "Yes, her."

Now, two years later, he was in a frenzy. His wife had not been home when he returned from the lab early in the morning. He entered the bedroom where she and the baby slept. All was neat and in place, but the closet door was open and there were several empty hangers. The car was gone; the stroller was gone. He waited all day for her return. Finally, the next morning, he realized she was gone too.

He went to his office and tried to work. He had hit a dead end in his theory. Once so promising, it now seemed to be pure folly. He stared at the blank screen on his computer. He didn't know what to do. He sat there all day wringing his hands. He went home to sleep. She had not returned. He went back to his lab office and stared at the blank screen. A day later, a knock on the office door roused him. It was Mayfield and a man in uniform.

He had lost her. She was gone, and now she had perished, and if not, she was as good as dead to him. He wanted her gone so he could work. Now his work was in the rubbish heap. He was alone, deserted. It was he who should have died, but he hadn't died. What to do? Where to go? His mind was in a jumble of images. Finding the note from his mother. Where did she go? Why did she go? A tennis court. Leaving defeated. Hearing the student tear down his thesis. Stopping his ears against the baby's cries. Coming home to a nice dinner with wine and music. Her. His thoughts raced about with no direction.

Chuck it, he thought. Just forget the whole rotten life. Go, go anywhere. Do something you always wanted to do. Live off the land. A bare existence. Back to essentials. Don't bother with people. No people.

When the dean suggested he take off a month to recover from the tragedy of losing his wife and child, for there had been no news of them, he agreed, wryly smiling to himself.

He took his money out of the bank and stuffed a gym bag with essentials. He went to the bus station, and boarded a southbound bus. Alton exited the northern university community he had lived in for twenty-five years without a backward glance.

Chapter 14

Rising from her nap, Lila realized she should get busy. It was past two in the afternoon of the first day of her new life. She called the desk for the name of a baby store in the area. Chloe needed a stroller, thing number one. The store was in the shopping center down the road where she found a huge array in every price range. She looked for a stroller easy to fold, sturdy, and comfortable, and sat Chloe in one for a trial stroll in the store while she looked at cribs. The child started jingling the beads on a rod next to the bar. "I'll take it," Lila said. "It's a cash sale, if that'll help."

The salesman asked her name. Lila hesitated. What had she told the car dealer? "It's Bronstein," she finally responded. He asked for her address. "I don't have one yet," she said apologetically. "I'm at the motel, but I'm looking for a place to rent. Would you possibly know of one?"

"Let me make a call, Mrs. Bronstein," he said smiling. "My aunt has a nice one-bedroom she's trying to rent, but it has to be the right person, you know, she's elderly."

"Would she mind the child?"

"Just a minute, I'll ask her."

He came back with a name and address on a piece of sales slip. "She's home, if you want to go over now and look at the place. She had a lovely home, but since her husband died and her children don't live nearby, she rents the top floor, I think mainly for the company. I believe she'd like you, and she said the child was a plus."

Lila's eyes welled up. Was this man an angel sent from heaven?

"I'll go over right now, please. Let me put the stroller in the trunk and get directions, I'm new in the area."

Lila pulled up to a small two-story house with a bit of lawn in front. Mrs. Ida Goldring was a thin, slightly bent woman with a friendly smile. She looked over the pretty young mother before her, noting her curly brown hair and the pendant hanging from a silver chain around her neck.

"That's a lovely *hamsa* you're wearing. What stone is that in the middle?"

Lila was taken aback. Then she remembered the good-luck pendant that Judith had given her. "It's a turquoise, I think," she said.

Ida Goldring smiled. "Lovely, and it's brought you *mazel*, I see, in this lovely child." She crouched down to greet Chloe in her new stroller.

"I'm afraid you have to go upstairs to see the place, Mrs. Bronstein. What is your first name? Mine is Ida."

"I'm Lila, and this is Chloe," Lila said. "We'll walk up. Chloe loves climbing stairs."

"I climb," Chloe said. It took a while, holding her mother's hand and getting a boost now and then, but she made it.

The rooms were clean but shabby. There was a small bedroom with a double bed and a washed-out quilt. A kitchen unit had been put against one wall of the living room, which included a table and four chairs, a sofa, and a rocker. The floor was covered in linoleum. It seemed rather cheerless to Lila, but the two windows, one in the bedroom and the double one in the living room, looked out on the house next door where she could see a swing set. "This place will do just fine," she told Mrs. Goldring. The rent was within the budget; she guessed it would last her six months. If she could find a teaching job, she'd be able to manage.

"If you don't mind, I will move in today if I can get your nephew to set up a crib here. And I'll need a high chair too."

"Lila, I'm pleased to have you. What about your husband? Will he be coming too?"

"That's the thing. We are basically separated. I don't expect him at all, from the sound of things."

Mrs. Goldring raised her eyebrows but shook her head as if to say "These modern marriages." Lila paid her two months' rent out of her stash of bills. Ida thanked her. "I do have a high chair in my basement," she said. "If you want it, it's yours." The three went downstairs and looked over the chair. Lila would clean it up, get a new cushion, and it would do for the present.

She called the salesman, now noting his name, Scott Goldring, and reminded him that the crib she had looked at with him would be fine. If he could have it brought over and put together, she'd go out and buy bedding and stuff, and she could be set up by dinnertime.

"My aunt and family go to synagogue on Friday nights, Mrs. Bronstein," he said brightly. "We'd be happy to have you join us."

Lila drew back in surprise. The name she gave must be Jewish. And the *hamsa* that Judith gave her confirmed it—they think I'm a Jew!

"Oh, my God," she said aloud, which she quickly converted into a response. "I'd be delighted." No one would find Lila Ostro, no religion, hiding as Lila Bronstein, Jew.

It's amazing, she told herself, but if I wanted a new identity, I've found one big-time.

Back to the shopping center she went, piling a new quilt, a half-price sale rug for Chloe to play on, a box of alphabet blocks for her, some colorful pillows for the sofa, and a soft throw for bed or sofa, as needed. She had not checked the heating system. It was beginning to be cold, and she hoped her landlady turned up the heat when necessary. She stocked up on bananas and fresh vegetables she could steam and mash for the child. As she was paying, Chloe spoke up.

"Car," she said, pointing to a plastic-wrapped tiny green car on the rack at the checkout counter.

Lila was amused. "You want the car, honey?"

"Car," Chloe said with certainty. Lila and the cashier smiled. She paid for the car and handed to Chloe who put it in the tray in her stroller.

She fed Chloe in the high chair. The child had been hauled around since the night before with just a nap; how would the little one behave in the temple? Ida said that the women with little children sat at the back with their strollers in case they had to go to classrooms to change or quiet a baby. Lila could wear slacks; the kids had their pajamas under their snowsuits. This was a very informal service.

Lila drove to the synagogue under Ida's direction. It was a small sanctuary, not half the size of the one she had been to with Judith. It was also very different. The men didn't wear skull caps, and the rabbi walked down from the pulpit to the congregation to give his sermon. Earlier, he asked the congregants to share any good news they had. "Only good news," he repeated to chuckles from the members. The outgoing salesman, Scott, rose to introduce Lila Bronstein and her baby Chloe to the gathering, pointing to them seated in the rear, explaining that she would be staying with his Aunt Ida.

The color rushed to Lila's cheeks, but as many in the congregation turned to look her over, she had the presence of mind to wave her hand. The other mothers introduced themselves in whispers, and one commented, "When you're ready, we have a wonderful pre-K here, and a Hebrew school too." Lila's eyes opened wide. It would be too amazing if they had an opening. Lila allowed that she was an early childhood schoolteacher and was looking for a position.

"I think there may be one," whispered Mimi Damrosh, one of the mothers. "We'll talk at the *Oneg*." A stab of fear ran through Lila. What was an *Oneg*? She'd soon be found out when they realized her ignorance.

Lila remembered that Judith had derided some of the members of her synagogue as being illiterate in their faith. "Totally assimilated Jews, they don't know anything," she complained. "They're here so they can have a big bar mitzvah party for their friends. But they'll find out that they have to attend services with their kids, and some do eventually find that they like the whole *megillah*," Judith laughed. Okay, that word she understood. Lila remembered they read the *Megillah* at a Purim party she attended with Judith and her children. She could guess that *megillah* meant the whole nine yards of the faith. She'd pass as one of those assimilated Jews.

The rabbi welcomed everyone to join at the *Oneg* following services that she discovered was a bountiful reception in the social hall in honor of the day of rest to come.

Her new acquaintance, chubby Mimi Damrosh, pulled Lila, rolling Chloe behind her, to the rabbi. "Lila is a pre-K teacher, Rabbi, what do you think of that!"

"Wonderful! Michael Gordon," he said, extending a hand. "Welcome to the Beth El community. We do have a maternity leave opening until June. Would you be interested?"

"Thank you, Rabbi. I'm thrilled to be here. I would be interested in a position," Lila said, adopting a businesslike demeanor. "I do have my credentials with me, sir."

"Oh, no 'sirs' around here. We're informal, a Reform congregation. Ours is a regular pre-K curriculum with the plus of introducing Judaism to our babes."

"I have to admit, Rabbi, that my Judaic background is very limited, but I would love to learn."

"Please, you'll come in Monday and we'll talk," Rabbi Gordon said, turning away to greet other congregants waiting to challenge his sermon. An athletic man with graying hair, he seemed happy and confident in his role, Lila thought, looking forward to their meeting.

They drove home, Lila in a blur of happiness. Ida said to leave the stroller in the corner of the foyer. Lila and Chloe hurried up the stairs. She closed the door to their rooms and eased the already slumbering child into her crib. Lila washed up, took a muscle relaxant for her lingering pain, and fell into the double bed.

"Ay, it's too soft, I'll have to get a bed board," she murmured, already half-asleep.

A streak of sunlight lit her face. She woke with a start, looking first at the crib. It was empty!

"Chloe!" she screamed. "Chloe, where are you?" She had visions of Alton. She threw off the quilt and padded into the living room.

"I play car!" There sat Chloe with blocks piled up, throwing the car at the wall she had created. She grinned at her mother, who burst into tears and laughter and ran to hug her.

"Come baby, phew, pooh. Let's get you a new diaper," she said, grateful for the messy chore and her brilliant child.

Chapter 15

On Monday morning, Lila called the synagogue. The rabbi invited her to bring her credentials and come on in; it was an emergency. Lila and Chloe arrived soon after. Rabbi Gordon looked over her college transcript and nodded. There was a letter of recommendation from the school principal where she had done her student teaching, and one from the school where she worked before taking the job at the university. She could not include the latest information, of course. If the rabbi should call for a reference, she would be undone. "These are impressive," Rabbi Gordon said politely. What had she been doing since her first teaching job? he wanted to know. She had married, she said, and they moved around, then she had Chloe. She came to the area because she had a brother in Pittsburgh. She hated to lie, especially to this man who seemed so trusting, so she kept her answers as vague as possible. The rabbi seemed unfazed by her nonspecific answers, or was he just desperate?

"Mrs. Bronstein, our teacher for the four-year-olds is pregnant. She's just been told she must stay in bed if she wants to carry to term. I was prepared to have a replacement for her by January, but now I need someone yesterday. The Israeli assistant teacher is holding the fort for the moment.

Come along, Mrs. Bronstein and Chloe, we'll visit the classroom."

They found Morah Shulamit. They called the teachers Morah, Lila understood, because she was introduced as Morah Lila. Shulamit was trying to shepherd her fourteen kids into a line so they could march down the narrow hall to music class. "*Shecket*, quiet and listen," she called to them, "line up please, you're blocking the whole hallway!" The kids were greeting Rabbi Gordon and were bunching together to talk to Chloe who kept calling, "School, school."

"Morah needs you to line up," the rabbi said in a serious voice, to no avail.

Lila approached Shulamit. "Ask them to put a finger on the wall," she whispered.

"*Yeladim*, each one put a finger on the wall!" called the teacher. The kids looked up and scrambled to find a space so they could touch the wall. Like magic, they were lined up. Shulamit beamed. Rabbi Gordan smiled. They entered a carpeted classroom. An older woman with a guitar asked the children to pick an instrument—a drum, a tambourine, or a chime—and to give a tambourine to little Chloe, who looked at it with wonder. While the music teacher began a song on her guitar, over the din, Rabbi Gordon explained the makeup of the school to Lila. He offered to take her to the Fours' classroom. As they began to wheel Chloe away, she called out, "No go, stay!" looking up at her mother.

"Chloe dear, we'll come back, let's go with the rabbi now."

"Keep the tambourine, Chloe," the rabbi said. And they began their tour.

They entered the now vacant classroom for the four-year-olds. The tart odor of poster paint touched Lila's nose, a familiar smell that made her smile. The wide windows opened to a vista of the temple garden bathed in sunlight. She saw there was a bathroom in the classroom. "Excellent," she murmured to the rabbi. In the Threes' classroom, the youngsters were busily at work when they entered. The kids were trying out designs with finger paints, their little fingers swirling paint on a wide sheet. "Oh-h," Chloe said with longing.

"I love it," Lila crooned to no one but herself. In the atmosphere of a place of learning, she felt serene and, at the same time, energized.

The threesome left the classroom after thanking the teacher and waving to the kids who raised dripping palms at them and giggling. Back in the rabbi's office, he chuckled. "I think Chloe would like our preschool, Mrs. Bronstein. And you look rearin' to go."

Lila grinned. "With Morah Shulamit offering the Hebrew, I feel confident I can handle the classroom, Rabbi Gordon. I'd be honored to join the community here."

"You'll need to have a physical before you can start. I'll give you the number of our school physician. I'd like you to begin this week if possible, on a trial basis, of course."

"I do have to find child care for Chloe, Rabbi. That may take some time. We've never been apart, but she loves being with other children."

The rabbi mentioned the Creche at the local YMCA. "They take infants up to two years of age. We can enroll Chloe here at two, but not before. Go over and check them out. If you want a recommendation for a sitter, I'll see what I can do. I understand you are new in town. Are you related to the department store Bronsteins, by the way?"

Lila drew in a breath. Who were they? "No, no," she said quickly. "Off we go to the Creche, Rabbi, it's not Jewish though."

"We all get along here, Lila, this is a small community. We help one another. We have two children in the four-year class who are not Jewish. One is Korean, and the other—well, the mother said she heard this was a good school and a little bit of 'Jewish' couldn't hurt. The Y will make a fuss around Christmas, but then Chloe will have Hanukkah here at temple. She'll be all right."

Lila thought the Creche was well staffed, but she was hesitant to leave Chloe all day. She agreed to a play program there twice a week. What did attract her was the well-equipped gym. She longed to get back to the exercise regimen that had kept her fit. She would sign up for gym membership as soon as she could find a capable sitter for Chloe and one of whom Ida would approve.

The next day, Rabbi Gordon sent her Rosa Santiago, a motherly woman who had been caring for an elderly congregant; Frieda Shapiro had just entered a nursing home. Rosa welcomed taking care of a young person for a change. She could drive Chloe to the Y, she said, and take walks to the playground a few blocks away.

Ida nodded. "I'll keep an eye, don't worry," she told Lila. Rosa stayed on during lunch, and Lila was pleased to see that Chloe was content to have Rosa put her down for her nap.

"I must run to the store, Rosa. I'll be right back, can you stay?"

"Of course, missus," Rosa answered. They discussed her wages and hours, and when that was settled, Lila went to the local bookstore. She needed a primer on Jewish practices but fast.

"This is a new, just-published book that should fill the bill," said the proprietor, handing her *Jewish Literacy* by Rabbi Joseph Telushkin. Lila looked at the table of contents and thumbed a few pages. The book was a lifesaver; it seemed to have all the basics.

"I'll take it," Lila said, breathing a sigh. She actually felt intense curiosity about the religious practices she was about to embark on, practices she had only touched upon in her friendship with Judith.

Later, at the doctor's office, she wondered if he could detect the lingering pain in her spine from the accident. When the doctor pressed his stethoscope to her back, she tried not to flinch. "A little achy there?" the doctor said.

Lila nodded.

"But you're fine. I'll call the rabbi."

Her arrangements were made the next day. She spoke to Rachel, the teacher resting at home, and got the rundown of the schedule. It was important to stay close to the routine as she could. Thursday, her first class, sounded easy. But Friday, the mom-to-be said to expect the Shabbat Mommy with her challah and for Shulamit to lead the *bruchas*. Lila listened with growing trepidation. She asked Rachel what was expected of her.

"It's like Shabbat at home. Get the knife and the cutting board from the kitchen, and the grape juice. I think it's Mimi Damrosh's turn. She'll cut the bread while you and Shula can lead the *bruchas* and then distribute the challah."

Yeah, right. Lila thought. Thank goodness she had stayed for Nathan's class that day; at least she had heard the blessings for wine and bread before. With a pang, she realized how she missed Judy, her boys, and even boisterous Harvey. Judy must be wreck thinking of her friend's terrible end.

After Chloe was in her crib for the night, Lila dug frantically into the Jewish literacy book, focusing on Shabbat and all its traditions to be ready for what might be her undoing on Friday.

Shulamit asked the rabbi for a moment of his time after her Shabbat duties were concluded. "This new teacher, Rabbi, she doesn't know zilch."

"Mrs. Bronstein is like a lot of American Jews," commented the rabbi. "They practice light Judaism, they don't know Hebrew, but they can be fervent Jews nonetheless. Morah Lila told me that she had little religion in her upbringing. We have to work along with her. She is a competent teacher."

"Rabbi, she told the class next week we'll study Thanksgiving. Is that a Jewish holiday? I don't think so."

"Shulamit, this is a regular American pre-K school. Thanksgiving is an American holiday that our children should understand. It is based on our tradition of the first settlers, pilgrims who came to America for religious freedom. Jews identify with that, okay?"

Shulamit shrugged. "I guess so."

The following week, Shulamit and the class learned about Thanksgiving through pictures and stories and the dried corn and vegetables that Lila brought to class. The two teachers shook their heads and smiled when a little girl asked, "Why did they have a party?" and the Korean boy answered, "Because Hanukkah was coming!"

Lila picked up on that to explain how the two were connected through the yearning for freedom to worship that brought the pilgrims to America, and Hanukkah, that celebrated the return of the temple from those who tried to destroy it. She also noted to the children that Thanksgiving was similar to the Jewish harvest festival of Sukkot that the pilgrims had read about in their bibles. (That explanation she got from Harvey Goldstein, who had made a point of proclaiming that theory during a Thanksgiving dinner at his and Judith's home. Thank you, Harvey, she said silently.) Shulamit seemed impressed with the explanation.

Three weeks later, the children were busy making Hanukkah menorahs, when the temple secretary opened the door. Lila was wanted in the rabbi's study. Lila wondered why whatever it was couldn't wait until after class.

When she entered, a slightly balding sandy-haired man in a tweed jacket rose. The rabbi said, "This is Dr. Shechter, Lila. His daughter, Andrea, is in your class." Lila's heart beat faster; had she done something to upset the child? Andrea seemed quiet lately, but she didn't know her long enough to make it a concern. Andrea was concentrating on working on her menorah when Lila was called away.

"Andrea's mother has died," said Dr. Shechter quietly. Lila put her hand to her chest.

"Oh! Doctor, I'm so sorry. Does Andrea know?"

"She knows her mother has been very sick. She saw her last week, and Susan just about bid her good-bye."

Lila's eyes filled with tears, and she wanted to reach out to the doctor who took out his handkerchief and covered his eyes.

"What can I do, Doctor?" she asked.

"Look, I want to keep things going on as before. We have a nice housekeeper—she's been with Andrea these last months of Susan's illness. Andrea will be out tomorrow for the funeral, but then, if she wants to go to school the next day, I would want her to."

"Of course, that is the best thing. I will be attentive to her moods but not make an issue of it with the students. Let Andrea lead. She seems like a very adjusted young person, but of course this—"

Rabbi Gordon stood to embrace the father. He nodded to Lila and asked that she bring Andrea to his study. She steadied herself before going into the classroom. What if this were me? she thought. Oh, how terrible for this child. When she approached Andrea, the little face looked up at her. "It's my mommy, isn't it?" she said paling. Lila hugged the child to her, but whispered brightly, "Daddy's here for you. We'll go to him, he's with Rabbi Gordon."

That evening, Ida had come upstairs and they were sharing a cup of tea and lamenting Susan Shechter's death, when Lila received a call from Dr. Shechter. "I hope I'm not imposing, Mrs. Bronstein, but Andrea wants you to come to the funeral."

"Oh, that sweet, dear child. It's in the middle of my day, but I'm sure the rabbi will let me. Do you have family members coming?"

"Yes we do. There will be a big crowd, I'm sure, and Susan's friends, who have been so attentive. But Andrea was crying, 'I want Morah Lila,' ay, I had to ask you."

"Well, of course I'll come. Please tell Andrea I'll be sitting in the back but I'll be there for her. I'm so new in the community. I don't want to intrude, but for Andrea . . ."

"Yeah, okay. Thanks then, good-bye," and he was off the phone.

"The poor man," Lila said, explaining the phone call to Ida. "He must be at his wits' end. I must call the rabbi." Ida said good night and slowly went down the stairs. Lila watched until she was safely in her own part of the house. Then closing the stairway door, she called the rabbi at his home and relayed the phone call.

"Yes, you should go. That's a mitzvah. It's so painful for Mort. He's a hematologist, you know—she had leukemia. He saves so many of his patients, but he couldn't save her. Believe me, they tried everything. I gave blood more than once. So we'll see you at eleven. Shulamit can supervise the dismissal and start the afternoon group if you're not back." He gave her directions to the funeral home, and she drove home to pick up Ida at ten the next morning.

Chapter 16

Lila had been to only one funeral. Her mother had not wanted a fuss, so there had been a graveside service. The only other funeral she had gone to was when a faculty member had died and she attended a lengthy, dreary service. Lila worried for little Andrea, hoping it would not be grim. But Michael Gordon spoke lovingly of Susan Shechter and how brave Andrea was, visiting her mom, making cards for her with a million hearts. A soft laugh rolled through the chapel. Mort Shechter looked down at his little daughter; she was smiling. Then there was a Hebrew prayer. Everyone said the words standing in place. The cantor sang a mournful song, and people were wiping their eyes. Directions were given to those who were going to the cemetery and the times when people could visit during the six days of mourning.

Lila hoped the child would be spared further ceremony. Then the casket was escorted up the aisle by six men whom Lila assumed were relatives and friends. Andrea and Mort came up the aisle holding hands with Flora the housekeeper following. Everyone else waited, filing out behind the family row by row. Lila bent down to embrace Andrea when she reached her row. The child took Lila's hand.

"Can my morah please come home with me?" she begged.

"Andrea is going home now," Dr. Shechter explained.

"Please come too," Andrea said as they paused before her.

"Would you be able to?" asked the father. Lila nodded.

"I must find a ride for Ida Goldring," Lila said, appealing to the father. A man in the aisle stepped forward. "I'll see that Ida has a ride."

"Thanks, Ben," said the doctor. Lila and Andrea and Flora left together in Lila's car.

Andrea was in school the next day, looking uncertain. Several children, whose parents had been at the funeral, looked shyly at her. "We are so glad all our class is here today," Lila said brightly. "Shulamit, would you lead us in a blessing, please."

"A *Shehecheyanu* would be good," Shulamit announced, "because we are grateful to be all here and together again in this place, please repeat after me." The blessing recited, Lila's class resumed its regular routine.

Not long after, Rabbi Gordon informed Lila that he was very pleased with her work and she was welcome to become a member of the school's permanent staff. She gratefully accepted. He reminded her that he and his wife and kids hosted an open house on the Sunday afternoon during Hanukkah and members and staff were welcome to attend. Chloe and Lila came with a bowl of cut-up fruit. Mimi Damrosh, the mother who had introduced her to the rabbi, hugged Lila, and several parents stopped by to tell her their children were enjoying and learning in her class. She also met several single mothers who invited her to take part in their round-robin on alternate Sundays; two mothers sat for all the kids, while three others went out for a festive lunch. Lila said she'd be delighted to join.

Mort Shechter was suddenly standing before her, ending her reverie. "Mrs. Bronstein, I have wanted to thank you for going home with Andrea that day. It was a great solace to me. She really doesn't know her aunt that well. She lives in Pittsburgh. So you were a godsend."

"Oh, Doctor. I'm so happy how well Andrea is doing. And I was most pleased to help. And please call me Lila."

"After *Shloshim*, perhaps I can take you and your husband to dinner to show my appreciation." Lila was tongue-tied for the moment. What was *Shloshim*? And what should she say?

"That's very thoughtful, but not at all necessary," she stumbled out. "Thanks, anyway." Dr. Shechter bent his head, and the two turned away.

She looked at the doctor, now greeting several congregants. He seemed to be listening politely. He had such a quiet sadness about him.

She would enjoy having dinner with him, having an adult conversation. He was so solid-looking—oh, how she would love to make him smile. Still, she thought her response was appropriate. Perhaps *Shloshim* was a year. Who knows? She'd just have to wait. Stop it, she told herself. You're disgusting. The man's wife has just died, and he wouldn't ask you to dinner if he didn't think you had a husband. Nevertheless, she dove into her *Jewish Literacy* when she came home and found that *Shloshim* meant thirty days; after that, a person could go about his or her usual activities while still observing eleven months of mourning.

She decided to make the slightly hostile Shulamit her confidant. "Shulamit, you'll have to help me with some of these terms. *Bimah* I've got, but now the rabbi is saying something—'Hag samcha'?"

Shulamit, in her patronizing way, corrected the pronunciation of *Hag Sam-ay-ach*, happy holiday. Lila repeated the phrase to her several times until she got it right. "Oh, Shulamit, thank you so much." Shulamit screwed up her face and shrugged. She knows I'm a fraud, Lila thought with a pang. But just as suddenly, she lifted her head in pride. What'll be will be. Meanwhile, I'm making progress in my literacy book and finding out the most incredible things about what is really a whole Jewish civilization.

Chloe was blooming, running around, talking in sentence bursts that now included verbs. She even was parroting some Spanish words from Rosa that she heard her speak to other Latin-American nannies in the playground. When Chloe played with alphabet blocks on the rug, she and Rosa would recite the letters on each one. "Chloe is learning from me, and I'm learning from her," said the cheerful woman. Chloe is way ahead of her age group, Lila realized. It must be Alton's genius gene.

Lila and Chloe settled into their new community of St. George. It was a nicely integrated town. A button factory, a tool-and-die machine shop, and a sprawling pharmaceutical company represented the manufacturing sector. The hospital, situated between St. George and the city of Cortland, employed others. There was a nursing home, a business college, a high school, and a number of private schools. The downtown was still vibrant, with cafés, several restaurants, and shops of all kinds. Except for two anchor buildings on the main street, no structure was more than three stories high so that the sun was always in the thoroughfare at one side or another. A glass-clad office building rose higher at one end of the street, with a small department store in an old Beaux Arts building at the other. A supermarket and a movie theater were in the mall where she had purchased her stroller. Lila liked the town; it was walkable and lively. I guess I'm just a small-town girl, she thought, comparing herself with her college classmates who now lived in New York City.

The first Sunday she took part in the round-robin lunch date, she brought Chloe to Mimi's home. It was in a section of town she hadn't visited before.

Temple Beth El was in a residential area with fine homes and well-kept lawns. Ida's area was less grand, but the houses and grounds looked cared for. Mimi lived on a street with several vacant houses with overgrown lots. The small houses looked tired and worn. Mimi's house had peeling paint, and the concrete front steps needed repairing. Mimi stood at the open door and ushered Lila and Chloe in with her usual warm greeting. They entered a living room strewn with toys, jackets, and hats. Mimi's one-year-old, Sarah, and David, the six-year-old, was helping his sister with a puzzle while munching a soft pretzel. David looked up and smiled at Lila. After taking off her own jacket, Lila stuffed Chloe's hat and jacket in her coat sleeve to keep them together in the confusing array. Chloe toddled over to the children and sat down near them, watching them holding the wooden pieces of the puzzle. Sarah fumbled, trying to place hers in the open space. David straightened it out for her. Then it dropped in. David handed a piece to Chloe. She studied the puzzle for a moment and then correctly placed it.

"Look at that, Sarah. Chloe put it in straight. Now you try this one," he said, putting a new shape in Sarah's chubby hand.

Lila kept one eye on Chloe as she greeted three other mothers with their little ones. She hadn't given much thought to the single women in the congregation, but now her eyes were opened. One mother, she learned, had conceived a child through a sperm bank. Another was married to a man who was studying in Israel for an indeterminate period. A third was divorced. Mimi was a widow. Her husband had

had a stroke and died while she was pregnant. Lila wasn't the only troubled person in that room. Her heart went out to these women who were, like her, braving the difficulties of parenthood alone.

After everything was arranged among the women and the children, special food for one youngster given to Mimi and extra diapers handed to Lila, the three women were free to go. They left, chatting and smiling, joyful to have a couple of carefree hours.

Lila and Mimi kept the children amused, changing diapers and helping them wash up. They gathered the six kids around the kitchen table for mashed vegetables, milk, and ice cream. Chloe was all eyes. She gobbled up her food, and when the meal ended and they started to sing "Inky, Dinky Spider," she concentrated as she tried to imitate her mother's finger play that went with the song. The kids sprawled on the floor, several napping on towels Mimi spread out for them. The mothers returned, refreshed, promising Lila and Mimi a lunch out two weeks hence.

Everyone has troubles, Lila thought. These women are not afraid to share their burdens. I cannot, yet my crazy idea has brought me the joy I never had known in my old life. She had the warm feeling that she belonged where she was, that she could help these women and herself. It's so meaningful here for me, I can't give it up. Not yet, she told herself. It's like a drug; I want more.

Spring was in the air now. The trees were budding, the pale yellow leaves gently unfolding and greening as the days warmed. Cement pots along the main street were brimming with impatiens. Rachel had had her baby, a little girl, and was feeling fine but not opting to return to teaching. "The baby is too much fun," she told Lila, who was relieved that she would not be displaced.

June was approaching. Lila could be employed all summer in the day camp program for local children. There was ample room for outdoor play on the temple grounds, and older kids were welcome to join the camp. Trampolines were brought out, and under Lila's supervision, the older kids were learning the beginnings of gymnastics, tumbling on the trampoline, doing handsprings on the lawn, swinging on the bars of the jungle gym. Lila gloried in watching the little athletes.

Twice a week the fours to sevens were taken to swimming lessons and fun at the Y pool, while she stayed back to supervise the younger ones. Now past two years old, Chloe joined the temple camp, playing roll-the-ball or sitting on her little rug in the classroom to listen to stories in the picture books. In the fall, she would enroll in the preschool. Lila wouldn't need Rosa full-time from then on. Rosa agreed to come in several evenings a week to babysit.

Mort Shechter brought Andrea to camp and repeated his invitation to take Lila and her husband to dinner. She decided to be forthright in her response. "Mort, my husband and I are separated. He doesn't live here. But I thank you for your nice thought." Mort seemed confused. He had had a different notion of Lila. Now he looked at her anew.

"Well," he said after a moment, "perhaps you and Chloe could join us on an outing during the summer. Now that Andrea has graduated to the fives,"—he chuckled at that—"there should be no conflict of interest. Also, I'd like your opinion of the next step, private or public school for her. I wish there was a kindergarten here. I've spoken to the rabbi about it, but he said this year was too soon to make it possible."

"You know I'm pretty new to the community, Doctor, but I'll make some inquiries for you among the other teachers about schools. You might ask your friends and colleagues for their experiences."

"Good idea. I'll call you, if I may."

Lila smiled at him and nodded with warmth. Still, she had no illusions. The women would be after him pronto, a nice-looking guy with a substantial practice and a lovely home. She didn't stand a chance, she told herself. Be realistic, you can't get serious with anyone in this role you've chosen for yourself.

Over the summer, father and daughter and mother and daughter went on many outings together. They enjoyed the county fair, apple picking, a visit to a lake, and cookouts at Mort and Andrea's home. Mort was an expert on the grill. Lila watched from her Adirondack chair in the backyard as he worked. He is so manly and graceful at all he does, she thought, I almost wish I had a blood disease so I could go to him. She began laughing.

"What?" asked Mort. Lila shook her head. "I'll get the fixings for you, Mort," she answered, going to the kitchen, her face wreathed in a grin. Just being near him gives me such a glow, she realized.

What a lovely Sunday it was. Andrea played teacher with Chloe, who was enchanted with Andrea's playhouse under a tree and ate up everything the older child had to offer. But she and Mort were never alone.

In the fall, he surprised her by inviting her to dinner. They shared stories about their daughters and discussed her school and he his practice. Mort asked her how she liked the temple, he called it. He had been brought up in the Conservative branch of Judaism, as had her friend Judith, but bowing to his wife's preference, they joined the Reform congregation.

Lila said she absolutely loved the congregation, the rabbi, the school. "I experience a sense of joy when I am in the temple. Being part of the group makes me feel more alive, especially when we talk of social issues. Where else can you have a civilized conversation each week about the state of the world? Rabbi Gordon weaves what's current into his remarks on the Torah portion. He's amazing.

"I admit I have a hard time believing the concept in the Bible of God as an angry male personification," she went on, responding to the questions that her study of the Bible was raising. "Still, I love that the ancient superstars argue with God." They both smiled at this.

"You can imagine, as a person imbued with the scientific method, I too have trouble," Mort said. "Even as a kid I couldn't believe in the words I was to read for my bar mitzvah." he grinned at the memory. "I told my mother that I didn't want to be in a bar mitzvah because I didn't believe in God and all the prayers that said God had done so much for us and we should love him. She hustled me over to the rabbi that day. The party was all arranged, and the whole house was in a fever of plans. Canceling my bar mitzvah would be a major tragedy. I was scared to death to go to the rabbi. How was I going to defend myself for such heresy?" Lila caught her lip in anticipation.

"The rabbi sat me down with the door closed and explained that's not why I was having a bar mitzvah. 'It's to agree to become part of a team, to carry on a heritage that goes back thousands of years devoted to making the world a better place,' he said. Later, when I have more life experiences, he told me, I may understand God in a different way I couldn't do as yet. Well, I liked that, my family breathed a sigh of relief, and I had a happy bar mitzvah."

Lila smiled at him, trying to picture the boy and the rabbi in this fraught encounter. "So did your mature self find God?" Lila smirked.

"You don't have to believe in God to be Jewish, Lila. We're a kollel, a holy community devoted to healing the world. Our Jewish sense of belonging can encompass all facets of belief. When I am in the synagogue and we thank God for taking us out of Egypt, I thank my grandfather for leaving Prussia and coming to America. I thank God for all my blessings—Andrea, Susan and my parents, may they rest, my profession, my new friend." He smiled at Lila. She held her breath and felt the blood rush to her cheeks.

"How lovely," she managed to whisper.

"But, Lila," Mort said soberly, "once, as an intern, I was doing a bone marrow transplant on a patient, and I couldn't aspirate him. I remember saying 'Please God, help me.' That did steady me. For that moment, I guess, I let myself imagine there was something all-knowing guiding me. I tried again with a surer hand, and it went smoothly. It's a mystery, really, beyond my comprehension. I don't put down people that truly believe, I think that's a gift. But more than that, I feel we Jews have made so many contributions, I must do my part in continuing our heritage. Our Torah, the Bible, has, for centuries, been guiding mankind on how to live. Forget the battles and that stuff. It's the message of decent treatment of our fellow man that counts. And don't laugh, but humans are such a small speck in the universe, it helps to center me to think I am a descendant of those ancients that created our Bible. It makes me less of a speck. And now, with the Hubble's revelations that there are other worlds beyond ours it's more than a human can grasp." He laughed. "That's pretty incoherent, isn't it? But it is how I feel. I've never really said this before." He looked at her shyly.

Lila shook her head. "It's a wonderful to hear your thoughts." And inside she was tingling. How marvelous to converse with a man who has his warmth and compassion.

Her upbringing was loving but so spare, she reflected. She needed to add her own thoughts to Mort's.

"We can't invent everything afresh," Lila said with conviction, having missed a way to mark her mother's death and burial in the lonely cemetery. "Life cycle rituals, in every faith, give us a basis for appreciating the happenings in everyday life. And in Judaism, to do things together, both in happy and sad times, is a great solace. Judaism isn't only the Holocaust, persecution and Anti-Semitism, as I was led to believe. It can be fun. The festivals, the singing, the hora, the spirit in this congregation all give me a community that I need so desperately." A stop sign flashed before her. Don't go there! He's never asked about your family. You don't want to lie. Change the subject.

She asked Mort why he chose hematology as a specialty. His father had a clothing factory outside Pittsburgh and wanted Mort to join the business. But he loved the sciences, and when he was admitted to medical school, his father was proud of him.

"My brother-in-law, Leonard Moss, was willing to take over. So I was free to follow my path. In medical school, we had rotations in each specialty. My mentor was a charismatic guy who described the advances about to be made in his specialty, hematology. I was hooked. I also like lab work, and this specialty combines both. But," he sighed, "the advances he spoke of were not soon enough to save my wife."

She touched the sleeve on Mort's jacket in sympathy. He smiled at her. They had never shared intimate thoughts before, but she could see Mort was still in mourning. She yearned to tell Mort about her Introduction to Judaism program she had started with the rabbi at a synagogue in Cortland, but held back. She'd have to reveal the whole *megillah,* as they say. And with his reluctance to go forward, she didn't want to burden him with her troubles and deceptions.

She had told no one, but she had begun spending two evenings a month in Cortland with a Conservative rabbi who was preparing her to become a Jew by Choice, in addition to the one evening a week learning the basics of the faith.

Why, the rabbi had asked, did she want to become a Jew? Her answer was the truth: she had had no religion before; her family never had a Christmas tree or a wreath on the door. They were declared atheists. They didn't attend the church they had been born into. She explained to the rabbi that her working with Jews and celebrating holidays with them had given her a heightened sense of the wonders of existence.

"I think the symbols, the stories, have so much to tell us about life. I love the concept that we are here to help heal the world. I have a strong urge to belong to something so meaningful."

She still had much to learn, the rabbi said after their second private session, but he complimented her—"I think you are capable of seeing life through Jewish eyes." She beamed. Maybe, someday, Shulamit would accept her.

Rabbi Newman was a photographer. His study at the synagogue had color photos of travels he and his wife had taken. Waiting for him one evening, Lila admired his views of national parks that she recognized—the sculptured sandstone towers of Bryce Canyon, the sun coming up on the great cleft that was the Grand Canyon. She had visited these sites with her parents. There were shots along the Smoky Mountains. One photo on the wall was of a chair made of willows, the reeds gracefully bent into circular shapes. She commented on the beauty of the chair to him.

"I took that in Asheville last year, in a shop in the town. The chair is really a work of art. I wanted to purchase it, but it was already sold. I have one on order though. My wife wants it at home when it comes. You'll come over to see it," he said a smile lighting his face. Then they sat at his small conference table and set to work.

Lila told no one of her twice-a-month journey to Cortland. Ida Goldring did notice the Hebrew workbook she saw on Lila's table when she was upstairs visiting. Lila laughed. "I want to know as much as my students."

Mort and Lila met almost weekly for dinner, the nights varied but always during the week. He devoted his weekends to Andrea when Flora was off. Lila and Mort mused about politics, coming elections, the booming economy, and their work. She told Mort that she had had a frustrating conversation with a child's mother that day.

"We're putting on a play about Passover, so this mother calls and says she doesn't want her son to be a slave in the play." Mort was chewing on his mouthful, but he burst out laughing, coughing into his napkin. "'Why can't he be Aaron? That would be a suitable part for him,' she tells me. I told her Moses's brother is not a person in the play, that the parts are all given out. Well, she repeats, her son is not to be a slave." Mort doubles up again.

"This woman is already working on getting her son into the Ivies," he laughed. "So how did you handle it?"

Lila was grinning from ear to ear. She had made her widower laugh. "I told her that he would play the part, or not be in the play. She wouldn't do that to him, she said, so she gave in. I told her that she would be very pleased with what she saw. I didn't tell her that her son was actually, after God and Moses, the hero of the story. He is Nachshon, the slave that was not afraid to enter the sea while the others hesitated."

"Why not put her mind at ease?" Mort asked, chuckling.

"It was the principle of the thing," Lila said with determination. "She had to agree to be part of the communal effort, not because her son had a special role."

Mort sat back, smiling. "That's a lovely story. And Nachshon, I never heard of him before."

Lila blushed. She had been doing a lot of reading, and she felt rewarded.

Despite their frank talk about religion, they both steered away from personal matters—Mort, she surmised, because he was trying to make peace with Susan's passing, and Lila, because she had so many secrets. They shoulder-hugged when they parted but pulled away. Lila felt her heart sink that Mort was so reticent. She longed to have him turn his face toward her and taste his lips with their funny crooked smile.

They often arranged to go to synagogue together, taking Ida along. Their girls went to the classroom where the teens did babysitting during services. Later, the kids trouped in for the final songs. Lila was torn between laughter and tears to see her little daughter climb the steps to the *bimah*. Mort took them home to Ida's place, and it was all very proper, with Mort and Andrea calling "Shabbat shalom," echoed by Chloe, Lila and Ida, and then driving away.

By spring, with the congregants getting used to seeing them together, Mort and Lila began joining other couples at temple events. It was accepted that Lila was in the process of getting a divorce and Mort was befriending her.

Mort Shechter didn't want to pry or perhaps lead her to expect that his intentions were serious, but he did want to know how her divorce was proceeding. He was uncomfortable dating a married woman. Lila used the vague card again. He went along with it because he so enjoyed her company, and didn't renew his question. She must feel awkward too, being in marital limbo. But Lila knew that she'd have to contact Alton. Let me be a Jew first, she thought. That will make me feel more solid so I can withstand the blows from Alton that will follow.

The second summer of their relationship, Mort took Andrea on a trip to Alaska. Lila missed him terribly. What am I going to do? she asked herself in anguish. I desperately want to be close to him, not because he's a man paying attention to me, I've asked myself that. No, it's because the chemistry is overwhelming me. I kiss my pillow at night and imagine it's him. I admire him too—he's kind, he can be funny, he is so capable, and I just want to snuggle with him and make him happy again.

I feel I can be a helpmate to him too. He agrees to be on call when he's supposed to be off. He is always willing to help out a fellow physician. He's too kind and can be taken advantage of—yes, like I am doing to him right now, wretch that I am. I still have months of study to be confirmed as a Jew. Can I wait that long to end this charade?

Rabbi Newman called on Wednesday afternoon to ask Lila to meet at his home the next evening. He sounded tired, and Lila asked if he wanted to put off their appointment.

"No," he said. "I'm okay. I just don't want to drive to the synagogue. My house will be fine, and you can see my Asheville chair."

The door was ajar when she approached the house. "Come in," the rabbi called from somewhere inside. She found him in a small study lined with books. "My wife is at a town meeting," the rabbi said. "Go see the chair. It's in the living room."

The rocker, an intriguing weave of reeds and branches, stood by the fireplace. Suddenly a stab of fear shot through her. Hadn't Alton said he wanted to make a chair? *Preposterous*, she told herself, he's in his lab awash in numbers.

Almost without thinking, she upended the rocker, looking for a signature. There was a plaque on the underside. Her heart stopped. She leaned close to the inscription. The small metal tab read "Jan Polski, Chairmaker." Lila laughed and breathed a sigh of relief.

"What a wonderful creation," she smiled to the rabbi. He looked far away. He hadn't gotten up from his seat at a table in his study to greet her. She was concerned about him, but he insisted on going over her readings in a volume on the history of the Jews. They were discussing the Crusades when suddenly his head dropped to his chest.

"Rabbi!" she called. He didn't answer. Her first thought was a heart attack. She knew CPR and rose to open his collar. She fumbled for the phone on his desk and called 911.

The operator told her to start CPR if she could and leave the door to the house open.

The rabbi's chair swiveled, and exerting all her strength, his head resting on her chest, she was able to ease him slowly to the rug on the floor.

She tilted his head backward to open the airway. She ran to fling open the front door and back again to the rabbi. She began pumping his chest. He sputtered. Oh, thank God, Lila thought, he's breathing! She heard the siren coming closer. Two paramedics strode inside. She sat back breathless. The EMTs took over. They placed an oxygen mask on the rabbi's face while Lila answered as many questions as she could. The phone rang. It was the rabbi's wife, asking how their session was going. Lila, calming herself, explained the rabbi was awake and breathing but the paramedics would be taking him to the hospital.

She handed the phone to the lieutenant in charge who questioned the wife and then spoke in an upbeat voice to Mrs. Newman, suggesting she meet her husband in the emergency room. She wanted to speak to her husband if she could.

He was already on the gurney, but Lila managed to pull the receiver over to him.

"I'm okay, honey," he whispered.

The lieutenant took the phone away. "We're on our way," he said, handing the phone to Lila. "His wife wants to speak to you."

"Are you Rabbi's pupil?"

"Yes, Mrs. Newman, I am."

"Well, thank God you were there. I shouldn't have left him. He's so obstinate . . . I better go. Thank you, thank you."

After her traumatic week, Lila was speechless with joy when Mort called from Denali on Sunday. Her mouth was half-open in wonder listening to him enthuse about the bear they had seen with her cubs on a ride around the majestic mountain. Andrea was a great companion, still, he said, they both wished she and Chloe were with them. "I wish it too," Andrea allowed herself to murmur.

"We're leaving today," Mort said. "Monday for dinner? Just us."

Lila was practically weeping with joy.

That fall, Mort took the children, Lila, and Flora to a holiday fair at a community center near Pittsburgh. He bought tickets for the children and Flora to see a puppet show.

Mort said, "We can stroll around while they are there. I want to show you the dragon's den—too scary for the kids."

They entered a dark tent and carefully made out the steps down to a kind of pit. There was a coin machine that would allow one person at a time to look into a window. Mort put two quarters in the machine and instructed Lila to peer inside the lens. Suddenly, the lights blazed, raucous music sounded, and in the tiny window, a huge dragon writhed toward her. She bent back startled and laughed. Mort took her place at the window. She saw the wonder on his face as he looked at the papier-mâché creature. This serious-minded doctor was still a little boy at heart, she realized with joy. Impulsively, she pecked him on the cheek. The lights went out on the screen. She felt Mort's arms around her, his voice in her ear.

"I'm so crazy about you, Lila, I can't hold back any longer." Their lips met with a groan, and they clutched each other frantically, kissing each other over and over, until they heard giggles and footsteps on the stairs. They staggered outside, arms around each other. The past, the future disappeared for both of them. This was now.

Unbeknownst to Lila, as they were busy picking up their children, a ten-year-old boy had gripped his father's hand coming out of the puppet show. "Daddy, I saw Aunt Lila!"

His father frowned. "It must have been someone who reminded you of her, son," he said gently. "I know," Brett whispered. "Aunt Lila's dead."

Chloe was past three, so there was no reason not to let her sleep over at Andrea's occasionally with trusty Flora in charge. Lila brought Mort to her little apartment so they could be alone, but their conversation, laughing, and lovemaking was constrained, afraid to disturb Ida downstairs. Mort talked in quiet tones about his week.

"I had a horrible task yesterday. We had not yet developed the testing of blood for the HIV virus before 1985. Of course after that, all blood was tested, but some people earlier received tainted blood. I had to reveal to a patient that had recently come to me, a hemophiliac, that he had AIDS as a result of tainted blood. This person depended on blood transfusions to live. A total innocent. He was just one of the victims of that era. Arthur Ashe, you remember, the tennis ace, was another." He shook his head. "The man was bereft. He has a wife and children."

"That must have been so hard," Lila said. "But there are regimens now?"

"Yes, and we'll work to help him." He smiled at her. "You always make the sun shine for me, Lila."

Mort said that he and Susan had been dating since high school. After his first year in medical school, Susan's father approached his father asking what Mort's intentions were.

"To be honest, I didn't know myself. We had become a habit. I realized it would cruel to just break it off. So we got married. It was a good marriage, I like to think, and I loved her for giving me Andrea, but the last years were really hard. I've let her rest in peace this past year." He smiled at Lila with shining eyes.

"I love you, Mort," Lila breathed. They kissed and held each other, she smoothing his eyebrows and touching his face. He laughing and chasing her mouth for another kiss.

Mort broke off to ask her a question. Would she accompany him to a dinner dance at the country club two weeks hence?

"The medical staff, at the hospital, has this charity ball each year to raise funds for the hospital's neonatal wing. I've gone solo since Susan was ill. I'd like you to come with me to the dinner."

"Of course I will, dearest one," Lila said, pleased but worried. She had never been to any of the clubs in Flint. Her father was invited many times but made it a rule never to attend social functions of the union or management so as not to compromise his independent status. But her mother had gone to a luncheon one year and reported her dismay.

"You've never seen such largesse. The buffet had every sort of food, carving stations, a Chinese table, shrimp and oysters, soups of every color. Women took plates full, picking at each selection, leaving half over. After I took a dessert—they were beautiful—our hostess brought over a dish of more desserts to be shared. Hardly any of them were touched. It almost made me cry when I think of the hungry." That report had stayed with Lila. She was curious but uncertain.

"How dressy is it?" she asked.

"Well, the men wear tuxes but the women wear whatever—long, short, I don't know." He looked at her concerned.

"That's okay, Mort. It's time I bought a new dress, it'll be fun." Lila felt a certain thrill in going shopping for something frivolous like a party, dressing to please him. She found one in the department store in Cortland that fit her perfectly. Over it she would toss her black sweater.

The night of the dinner dance, Chloe and Ida were all eyes as she paraded before them in her satin burgundy cocktail dress. "You look just lovely, Lila," smiled Ida. "But, please, don't be offended, the *hamsa* doesn't go. Please allow me to lend you my pearls. I have no place to wear my things any more. They are crying to be let out of the box." With that she went down to her bedroom, returning with a strand of fat shining pearls.

"Oh, yes, Mom," Chloe said. "Put them on."

"Ida, you are too kind," Lila responded. "These look very valuable. I can't let you take the risk."

"There's no risk. See the clasp. It's foolproof. Let me put it on you."

Lila succumbed, not only to her daughter's eyes, wide with wonder, but to the realization that the pearls were the exact touch to complete her costume. She handed her *hamsa* necklace to Chloe to put on the night table. The bell rang at the downstairs door. They all trouped down to answer.

Rosa, the babysitter, entered followed by Mort, handsome in his tuxedo.

Mort's mouth fell open on seeing Lila. She'd only worn casual clothes or business dress with him. Now it was like discovering her for the first time.

"Am I okay?" Lila asked, giggling at his dazed expression.

"You're gorgeous!" he mouthed, while Ida looked on with a loving glance. Rosa and Chloe clapped their hands.

"Have a good time, missus," Rosa said. With kisses all around, the couple left.

Lila realized that she would be an object of scrutiny at the dinner dance. She'd be composed, she promised herself. She felt as if she were stepping onto a stage with all eyes upon her. But I mustn't act that way, I must be friendly and yet subdued, she counseled herself.

The large walnut-paneled dining room, lit by sparkling crystal chandeliers, was filled with round tables with flowers topping tall vases in the center. Several of Mort's colleagues were already at their assigned places, and Mort introduced Lila to the men and their wives. She received warm handshakes, and one of the men looked Lila over.

"Well, you took your time, old boy, but I see you've picked a winner." Lila smiled, keeping her to her script. She realized Mort was blushing. It was uncomfortable for him. Perhaps it was a mistake for him to invite her. It could only lead to embarrassing questions: Was it serious? When would they marry? She knew Mort; he couldn't dissemble. He'd never say they were "just friends." That would be such a lie.

When they were seated, as their table filled, the women, who all seemed to know each other, focused on Lila.

"It's nice to see Mort with someone," one of the wives said, opening up the conversation. "When did you two meet?"

"I was Andrea's teacher at the temple school," Lila said simply. "Our girls are friends, and Mort was kind enough to invite me to this special party." That's all she's getting, thought Lila, and it should be enough.

But it wasn't. Two of the women went off to the ladies' room to discuss Mort's date.

"She's a stunner," said one.

"She's not Jewish," said another.

"How do you know?" asked her confrere. "She works at the synagogue."

"Because I'm Irish and I know the stock. If she snags Mort, I'd be surprised. He's very devoted to his religion. But you never know." Hair and lipstick touched up, they returned to the table, smiling knowingly.

Lila kept a low profile throughout the dinner, but when she was asked what she thought of the Head Start program, she proceeded carefully.

"I believe it is a very important effort to bring children up to speed with their age-mates from more favorable backgrounds."

"But they say the progress is lost by grade two, if there was any," continued the questioner, Hugh Barnstable, a doctor of gastroenterology. "Some Head Starts are just glorified babysitting, I'm told."

Lila tried not to show anger at this statement, which she felt was a direct insult to her, meant to sting Mort. She saw him glance at her with a knitted brow. She needed to keep cool, to do him proud.

She sighed and nodded as a signal that the doctor was not altogether wrong, and then she struck.

"There are studies that indicate Head Start fades for kids that begin strong in the early grades and then fall back. What is not studied is how this group compares with kids from disadvantaged backgrounds who have not been in a program."

Lila saw that the questioning doctor was listening and so were the others. She smiled turning to her tablemates, as if asking permission to go on.

"Did you work in a Head Start program?" one woman asked.

"I taught kindergarten at an elementary school, but we advised the Head Start program at a local church. This was in Northern New York State, where unemployment was pervasive," she said thoughtfully, "the parents were striving to make a living. Head Start was a godsend for them. One mother told me her son behaved better at home since coming to the program. 'He makes his own bed and keeps his room in order,' she told me. She thought that was great. Once they get used to it, kids love a routine and order. Some have never had a story read to them, never held a blunt scissor before to cut out shapes, to measure with a ruler, to settle arguments peacefully, to learn the alphabet. We focused on vocabulary expansion. Kids have greater comprehension as they learn words from the stories that are read. How could they not have benefited? The church hosted seminars on parenting, we gave the mothers books for the children, some of the parents agreed to attend ESL classes. The involvement in the program had benefits for the whole family. I can't imagine that these three-, four-, and five-year-olds were not better off than they would be languishing at home all day.

"And to address your concerns, Doctor," Lila went on, "now that the Clinton administration has authorized more funds for Head Start, teachers will have to have a four-year college degree in early childhood education and salaries commensurate with teachers in the elementary grades.

That should improve the quality. Excuse me for running on like this."

"I see you feel deeply about the program," chimed in the doctor's wife. "I do hope it continues to improve," she said, staring down her husband, who chuckled.

"She always gets the last word," he said. "Thank you, eh, Lila. I just hope it's not one more boondoggle."

Then the talk turned to golf. The music resumed, and Mort asked Lila to dance.

"I'm not into fancy steps," he said, taking her in his arms. "You handled that well." He smiled at her when they were away from the table. "Hugh is a prick but an excellent diagnostician. I have to give him that."

"I loved parrying with him," Lila said. "I know, though, that you do feel uncomfortable introducing me to your friends?"

"It's just that you're not divorced. I can't say what I would wish to say until then, that I love you for all the world to know, and I want to make my life with you."

Lila looked into his eyes. "I'm so sorry," she said solemnly. "I beg you to be patient a while longer."

Chapter 17

Lila and Mort spoke almost every evening and had dinner together at a restaurant with their children at least once a week. Searching for privacy, the couple allowed themselves an occasional luxurious overnight respite at a bed-and-breakfast inn some distance away from St. George.

Making love with Mort was a revelation. He delighted in her body, touching and admiring each curve. She adored his manly form, smoothing the hair on his chest, tracing his features with a finger, kissing his neck, his throat, rolling with him entwined in a breathless embrace. "I'm in heaven," Lila whispered to Mort.

"It's pure rapture, isn't it, my darling girl?" No one had ever called her *darling* before.

It was on one of these retreats in April that on the TV in their room, a reporter was relaying the news that a third bomb had disabled a tractor-trailer in North Carolina and the police were actively engaged in seeking the culprit. Lila did not pay much attention to the report. Mort mumbled, "Another *meshugenah*," and turned to a different channel.

She was out for Sunday lunch with her women friends when she saw Mort at a table of men and women. Even though he was facing away from her, she knew it was his gray-blond hair at the back of his neck. She wished she were his companion. Her heart sank as he turned to speak to the person beside him. A handsome woman, somewhat older than Lila, responded casually and Mort nodded. Lila turned in her seat so he wouldn't see her. She tried to listen to the conversation at her table, a story about a hassle with the telephone company. The group laughed at what one of the women told the supervisor listening to her complaint. Lila hoped the burst of laughter wasn't so loud as to turn Mort's head. She was relieved when his party left without a backward glance.

She realized how unnatural her relationship was that she could not go over to Mort. He had another life to which she was not part of, nor did she have any right to be. She held her breath that their relationship would continue.

They enjoyed their casual dinners together as before, and now she and Chloe were included on Saturdays or Sundays. They often spent an afternoon at the Y playground and watched the children run around. One Sunday, Lila was watching Mimi's children for her and Mort and Andrea joined them. Lila made spaghetti and meat sauce on her two-burner stove. She tossed a salad and served brownies for dessert. She invited Ida to come up and join them, but she smiled and refused. While the four children played a board game and watched TV, Lila made coffee and doled out fruit salad to Mort as they chatted over the Sunday papers.

"This is so comfortable," he said, smiling at her. The children were laughing at something.

"Can we go too?" called Andrea.

"Mom, they're giving away ice cream, Mom," echoed Chloe. The two parents stood and looked at the screen. Indeed, children and adults were reaching toward a semi that seemed to be damaged, and a man, standing at the open doors, was handing out cartons of ice cream, some of it dripping.

"This is wild," David chimed in.

"Let's listen, kids," Mort said over the girls' cries of "See, See!"

"Ah, the refrigeration is damaged on the trailer and can't keep the ice cream frozen, so the owners are giving it away," Mort said.

"But it's in North Carolina, kids. Not here," Lila reported. To Mort, she whispered, "Can we take them out for ice cream? My fridge only has room for one ice tray."

So the party of six went out for a treat, the adults not mentioning the reality that someone had planted a bomb under the trailer that had blown apart the refrigeration.

But in North Carolina, the authorities were not amused at the ice cream giveaway. They were increasing their efforts to find the person trashing the trailers.

On the last morning in May, they were away to their retreat. Mort and Lila jogged together along the rail-trail, the abandoned site of the former Baltimore and Ohio railroad, before they had to head back. The morning mist was just beginning to lift off the fields. The air was redolent with the faint smell of fertilizer. This was farm country, and they breathed in spring air with its sweet and pungent odors as they bounced along a lane that was easy on the feet. Lila had to slow her pace to keep even with Mort.

"I'm not getting enough exercise," he confided. "I used to jog two miles every morning. Being mom and dad has taken its toll. I long for a normal household, Lila. Any news on the divorce?"

"I'll have some soon," she smiled, lifting her eyebrows at him. Her date with Rabbi Newman and the jury he would assemble had been set for June 9. He nodded in affirmation.

Can I wait that long? Lila goaded herself as she put Chloe to bed that evening. The moment I'm wholly Jewish, I'll tell him all. But should I do it now? I would have to contact Alton and to start the divorce papers. It'll be a whole muddle. I'll have to call Martin first, to let him know I'm alive. And my father, poor man. I hope I'm not too late. And Rabbi Gordon. Oh! What will they think of me? Lila put her hand to her face, covering her eyes. Oh, it's too awful what I have done. How can I ever square it? Well, I will just have to. Once I'm a Jew, I will, and that's not so far off. For the moment, what choice do I have? I must go on as I am, she admitted to herself, sighing. The sadness she felt forced her face into wrinkles of misery.

Chapter 18

The Hunt

As early at 1994, Sam Henderson of the highway patrol in Asheville, North Carolina, was looking into a series of explosions on semis hauling loaded trailers. The incidents took place over two years at different spots in a fifty-mile radius of Asheville. No one had been hurt, as the rigs had been parked and the blasts just strong enough to trash the trailers and the goods inside. Forensics established that the explosives were of the same type. A file of discharged drivers was checked. Some were working again. None were in the area at the time of the blasts.

"We've got to expand the search. Whoever is doing this, some crazy with a hate on big rigs—no matter, he's got to be stopped before he kills someone," declared Henderson. One more explosion had taken place since then.

Henderson began checking the accident record of persons injured in crashes with rigs hauling trailers. Several names came up. Personnel traced each one. Several fit the realm of probability. Each one would have to be investigated. A husband and wife had died in one accident. The search for next of kin was taking time. Alton Ostro, whose wife and daughter had been assumed to have died, became a likely suspect. No address for him was found. But the database listed him as a faculty member of Rush University. His university was contacted

"Dr. Ostro pulled out soon after the accident," Dr. Mayfield said. "He took his retirement savings and salary and resigned. He seemed to have lost interest in his work. It was very intense—his work, that is. And then the accident, I think it catapulted him into depression. I suggested a break and he took me up on it. I've never heard from him since. A great loss to science," Mayfield said. "It's a double tragedy, but I don't think he was of a violent nature or could perpetrate such actions as bombing trailers. Yet we'll help you in any way we can."

The bank in which Ostro's checks were deposited reported that the professor took his payout in cash. "It was over thirty thousand, we cautioned him about carrying all that cash," the head teller said. "I remember him because he was often late depositing his pay. He'd deliver rumpled checks dated six months earlier until he opted for direct deposit. He told me the cash wouldn't last long, and not to worry. Maybe he was going to Vegas," she chuckled.

Hard to trace cash, Henderson thought, making a mental note, and putting the amount on his pad. He awaited a photo of the professor.

"The guy was camera shy," Henderson's counterpart in the university town reported. "His employment application photo was missing. The only picture they could dredge up was of Ostro in a college yearbook from 1969."

The photo, when Henderson got it, showed a skinny kid with long hair covering half his forehead, an angular face, and a frown. Henderson had it duplicated and gave it to his deputy inspector, Paul Pierson. "It can't hurt to stop in some of the towns around Asheville and show this photo to the regular people. The police I've contacted don't recognize the guy. Of course, he's a lot older now. But give it a try. It's all we have so far."

Pierson had been a cop in New Jersey. He was near retirement. Is that why I got this dead-end assignment, he wondered, keep the old guy busy? But Pierson took the photo home, made copies, and tried to age the face. Ostro would be forty-five. He wasn't much of an artist, but he blanked out the hair over his forehead, added ears, rounded the chin, and added a few lines to the sides of his mouth and eyes. He made him partially bald in another copy and left the long hair. On his regular rounds, he'd take out the photos. People laughed at his renderings and shook their heads. In Perryville, he had a response.

Two codgers, lounging on a bench near the town library, were glad for a diversion. One thought he looked like the chairmaker.

"Who's that?" asked Pierson.

"Ah don't know his name, he's just known as the chayermaker around here," a man smoking a pipe answered. "Comes to the library now and then. Do you know his name, Vince?" he asked the other man, who grunted.

"Ah don't even think it looks like the chayermaker, you're dreamin', Jim Bob, as usual," Vince said.

"Still, I'd like to meet this chairmaker. Where can I find him?" Pierson asked, amused at the two old men.

"Oh, that, Ah can tell you," perked up Vince. "He consorts with Betty Lou over at the beauty salon." He pointed down the road and gave Pierson directions. "She'll tell you everythin' you want to know." Vince and Jim Bob grinned and wiggled their shoulders.

Pierson found the salon, with Betty Lou working on a patron. A plump friendly woman, she asked Pierson to wait on her porch. The elderly matron finally left, smiling at him for approval of her new coif. "Very pretty," he said, thinking he had done his good deed for the day.

"Yes," said Betty Lou, "how can Ah help you?"

"I'm looking for this person. Vince said you might know him."

"Who did Vince say he was?" she asked.

"The chairmaker."

Betty Lou looked closer at the three renderings. "Well, it does look somethin' like him, Ah could see where he thought there was a resemblance in this one," she said pointing the photo he had aged. She giggled.

"What is this gentleman to you, if I may ask," Pierson said.

"Well, to begin with, he's the fahther of mah daughter, Mollie."

"You're not married?"

"No, no, just good friends. It's no secret—Ah wanted a child before it got too late. Jan is just so talented and neat, Ah cottoned to him right away. He came to me for a haircut. Ah do men too. When Ah found out he was the one who bought the old barn and was livin' without electricity or runnin' water, Ah offered him the shower, and one thin' led to another."

Pierson nodded. "Tell me about him. His name is Jan what?" He wrote Jan Polski in his notebook.

"He told me he had been livin' in Canada," Betty continued. "Didn't like the cold. Moved here. Ah drove him home once, it was rainin' and he let me. He's very independent. Wants to live off the land. It's amazin' how he has solved makin' a barn a home. That's when Ah saw this gohgeous rockin' chayer he had made out of branches. Ah was so impressed, Ah told Alf Stoner about it—he sells thin's to tourists. Alf went out to the barn and got Jan to make him a chayer. Sold it the first thin' Saturday mornin' in his place in Asheville. After that, Jan was makin' one a week, gettin' good money too. He's very resourceful. What do you want with him, if he's the person you're lookin' for?"

A little girl running up the walk let go of a teenager's hand. "Here's my darlin' now," said Betty Lou, hugging the child to her.

"You've been very helpful, ma'am," said Pierson. "Let me inquire a little further before I bother Mr. Polski."

Now that he had a name, he had time to go to the bank in town before it closed. If the guy was selling chairs, he must have a bank account. Sure enough, he had one, but the manager said his account was confidential unless Pierson got a court order. The deputy decided to take the manager into his confidence, revealing that law enforcement was looking for the person who had bombed three semis so far.

The manager, a young blond woman, laughed. "Jan wouldn't hurt a fly. He's the meekest soul—part hippie, part recluse. He makes chairs out of branches he picks up in the woods around here. I have one. They're works of art."

"Sounds pretty far-fetched, I agree," said Pierson, "so keep it confidential. We don't want to trouble an innocent person. But I do want to meet this Jan. Please direct me."

"It's too late," said the manager, Josi Greenway. "He has no electricity, and it's getting dark. He goes to sleep when it's dark, gets up with the sun. Better come back in the morning when it's light. He'll see you then if he's not off collecting fallen branches."

Pierson nodded. He'd return with his captain on another day. Polski didn't sound too promising, but he was worth a look. There was still time to check the local hardware store before it closed in this one-horse town.

Pierson identified himself to the owner and then showed his photocopies. Ben Axelrod shook his head. "That could be anyone," he said smirking.

"Does Jan Polski do business with you?"

"Plenty. I put in a stack of batteries for him. Sold him tools. Uses a special glue I order for him. When he set up I got him a chemical toilet, a camper's lamp, all sorts of supplies."

"Does he buy fertilizer or magnets or pipe?"

"Nope, has his own compost heap. Shuns the stuff. Magnets, I'd remember if he did. What would he need pipe for, he has no plumbing."

"What's he use the glue for?"

"He won't use nails on his chairs. He's the chairmaker around here, you know. He glues what he has to, the rest he uses leather strips to bind the twigs and branches together. He's quite an artisan. Don't know why the highway patrol would be interested in him."

"Did you ever hear of the Trailer Trasher?" Pierson asked sighing.

"Oh, yeah, hah, hah, the chairmaker ain't no trailer trasher, I can tell you that. Never leaves the place. Just makes his chairs and stashes his money in the bank, and . . . has his weekly fling with Betty Lou at the beauty salon. You can catch him there on Mondays when she's closed."

"Well, thank you, Mr. Axelrod. Here's my card, just call me if you sell him any magnets or fertilizer, okay? And keep mum about what I told you. We don't want any gossip about this matter. I think you're right—it's too remote. We're looking at other possible perps." Axelrod shrugged, taking out his keys to lock up his now dark well-stocked store.

Pierson got in his car to head the thirty miles to his mountain home in Asheville. He was tired. He felt ridiculous bothering people in this small town on a wild goose chase. Could Alton Ostro, physicist, transform himself into Jan Polski, maker of chairs? It didn't seem likely. But if Ostro wanted to disappear, this would be a great disguise. Polski had moved to the area about the time Ostro left his post at the university. He opened his bank with some cash. Ostro took his payout in cash. It could be a coincidence, but in his long years on the job, he had found many coincidences that were not so coincidental.

Thank goodness they've got the Unabomber, he thought as he drove along. At least I don't have to worry that Alton Ostro is that misguided murderer. Perhaps Ostro related to what Ted Kosinski was doing. Both were professors. Both became recluses. Kosinski had a gripe against the machine age—this guy, whoever he is, has a death wish on sixteen-wheelers.

"What are you mumbling?" Arabella called from the kitchen as she heard her husband come into the house.

"I'm hanging up my hat and leaving my musings in it," Pierson said lightly, giving his wife a quick peck. "No talk about the job. I'll wash up and be with you in a minute. Looking to relax this weekend," he said, giving Arabella a Groucho Marx wink.

"Now, you," she said companionably. They had been married almost forty years. Both children were married also, and there was a grandbaby on the way.

On Saturday, Pierson proposed that they go into town, have lunch, and mosey around in the shops. "Lovely," said Arabella. "There's a new vegan restaurant I'd like to try, and the art galleries are fun."

Pierson made a secret grimace at that suggestion, but he'd go along with his wife's preferences. He always did. She soon realized why her husband had wanted to go into town, a five-mile ride on a winding hilly road to Asheville.

The city had a vibrant arts community. Art galleries lined Biltmore Avenue selling paintings, art glass, and ceramics. They saw no sign of the chair shop. They walked over to Pack Place, where the statue of Zebulon Vance overlooked the Plaza. Perhaps the chairs were in the art fair. A lively fair was in progress with artisans offering their wood carvings, pots, paintings, and a few doing portraits on the spot. A violinist, with an open case for donations, played stirring Russian melodies. The square was thronged with tourists. There were no chairs made of reeds to be seen.

Arabella thought her husband had a hidden agenda all along. If he wanted to find a chair shop, their best bet was to go back to Biltmore and ask, she suggested. There they were directed to a side street. A sign over a storefront, its letter burnt into wood, read, "Fine Mountain Crafts. Alfred Stoner, Proprietor."

"This is it, Arabella," he said opening the door for her. There was an array of chairs made of branches and twigs on the showroom floor, some of them labeled "Sold."

"These are so handsome," Arabella enthused. "Did you want us to have one, Paul?" Pierson ignored her and headed for a short bald man talking with a couple. "Mr. Stoner?" he asked.

"Yes, sir. Can I help you?"

"It's a private matter," Pierson said. Arabella frowned. She thought so. Stoner called over another clerk to help him with the sale. He excused himself to the customers.

"What is it?" he asked Pierson, who had taken out his ID.

"We're trying to get some information on Jan Polski, sir. Does he have a contract with you?"

"What are you, a tax official? I have no idea what he does with the money. I pay him in cash, and he puts it in the bank. And we have no contract. It's strictly a handshake deal."

"Do you pick up his chairs?"

"I've offered to, but he drags them into Perryville on a cart he built. Only time I've been out there is to deliver the seats and the rockers that the mill makes for him. He was crafting them himself, but it took too long—he has no electricity. Ridiculous. So I finally persuaded him that the seats should be made at the mill—he could finish them himself."

"He sounds ornery."

"No, he's the nicest, mildest guy but very reticent. I begged him to sign his chairs. He's got quite a name, you know. People come in here asking for a 'Polski chair.' The art society wanted him to give a lecture demonstration on twig furniture, but he refused. I finally had a small metal tag made with the name Jan Polski that I affix to a chair, really to protect him. Let me show you." Stoner upended a chair.

Arabella approached. "Do you want this one, Paul?" she asked with a twinkle in her eye.

"This is my wife," Pierson said. The two shook hands.

"Thank you so much for giving me time on your busy day," he said, steering his wife toward the front entrance.

"Some taking the weekend off," Arabella accused.

"Come on," he said grinning. "You're helping me with a case. Now let's do lunch."

Chapter 19

Tuesday morning was the soonest Sam Henderson and Paul Pierson, in plain clothes, could get out to the chair maker's barn. They found it in a clearing at the end of a long dirt road hemmed by willow and pine. The barn doors weren't open, so they went along to the back. There they saw a small garden fenced with chicken wire. The last of zucchini, tomatoes, and green beans looked healthy and cared for. Cords of wood were stacked under an open shed. The back door was ajar, but no one answered their call. They peeked inside. They saw a workbench with three vises attached on each side. Several pails held sawed branches of different lengths. On the wall were clamps holding an assortment of tools. A rocking chair made of branches and twigs sat in the corner near a partition. A plank table and a chair, also fashioned of branches, and a potbelly stove with a teapot on it made up the workshop cum residence as far as they could see. They did not enter; instead they explored the grounds, walking toward a narrow river. Further along on the bank, they saw a man hauling a net from the water. But it didn't hold a fish. It was full of long branches. Ah, the chairmaker, they thought.

He approached with his dripping load. The deputies hailed him; he paused, shifting his bundle. They identified themselves, requesting an interview.

"Let me get these branches in the vise while they're wet," Polski said. "Come inside."

The officers followed him and watched while he bent the pliable branches into arcs held by the vises on each side. Pierson occasionally gave him a hand. When he was through, he put water from a large cask into a basin, added hot water from the teapot, and washed his hands. The basin rested on a small table. Above it was a wooden chest with a rack for a towel and a mirror on its door. Then he sat on the edge of his bed and motioned to Henderson to take the chair and pulled out a polished tree stump from under another table near the stove. Now the officers saw the partition partially enclosed a bed covered with a patchwork quilt. Pierson surmised that the quilt was Betty Lou's work. In a far corner near the workbench was a closet that he assumed housed the chemical toilet. A window opposite the bed and the open door was the only source of light in the barn.

Pierson began. "I like your chairs. How long have you been at it?"

"I always thought a person should be able to make his own chair. Once I moved here, among these woods, I gave it a try," Polski said mildly. "I have to finish this one," he said pointing to a frame.

Pierson got the message: get on with it. He took out his three portraits. "Do you recognize this person?"

Henderson looked carefully at the chairmaker's face to see if he reddened or paled. Polski remained calm. He shrugged, pursed his lips, and shook his head. Pierson, who was looking at Polski's jawline closely and comparing it with the photo, realized the man had a fuller face. He said, "Some people thought this picture resembled you."

Polski smirked. He took the picture to his mirror and compared faces. "The nose is too small," he said. "I'll tell you who it does resemble—a guy I took in from the cold one night during that storm in March of '93."

"Yes?" said the two men, leaning forward.

"Well there was a snow storm, unexpected. I was fine, wrapped in the quilt reading by the lamp here when I heard a feeble knock at the door. I thought it might be an animal scratching. That was, what, three years ago, but I remember I called through the door and a male voice answered. I opened it and this chap covered with snow literally fell inside. He'd been lost, wandering in the woods. When he saw my light, he headed toward it. His boots were wet. That's the worst thing, wet feet. So I took them off first. He had a bedroll on his back. I propped him up on it and gave him some hot water to sip. He came around after a minute or two. Said he'd gotten off the bus before the storm and thought he'd camp in the woods. Woke to the storm and had been stumbling around ever since."

"Did he give you his name?" Henderson asked.

"Not really. He didn't talk much and neither did I."

"How long did he stay with you?"

"Until the storm abated, that night and the next. He insisted on sleeping in my loft. He had his bedroll and a zero-degrees sleeping bag, and he said he'd be comfortable. He used the toilet and washed up in the morning and shared my oatmeal with me, then went back upstairs."

"He stayed there all day?"

"Yup. I tramped through the snow to the river and caught me a nice trout. So I called up to him to come down and eat with me. He ate, went back upstairs. I heard him fiddling with something up there, the clank of metal, but then it became dark, and I guess he went to sleep like I usually do. The next day, his boots were dry, the storm had stopped, and he went on his way."

"In all that time, you never got his name?" said Henderson rather incredulously.

"Let me think, it was near three years ago. 'Ozzie,' I think he said. He stopped by in '95 again. He was riding a motorcycle. Asked me if I needed anything. That's when he looked like this picture. Said he was just traveling around. Kinda crazy, I thought."

"And you've never seen him since?" Henderson asked.

"Nope, can't say I have. But last April, I found a package at my door when I came back from town. It was this weird candle, really three candles braided together with three wicks. There was a large O on the package. I figured the Ozzie chap left it, maybe wanting to stay here again. He knows I use candles."

"Do you have the candle or the package?" asked Pierson hopefully.

"The candle was great—with the three wicks it burned bright as all get out. I used it up. The paper went in the stove. Why are you searching for this guy?"

"It's a police matter," Henderson said cagily. "Can you describe this man's height, his weight?"

"His hair was dark. He was kinda disjointed, awkward, I didn't figure him for a biker," Polski laughed. "Listen, I've got to get down to work. My wet branches need tending."

"Just estimate his height," Pierson urged.

"I dunno."

"Well, was he short? You saw him go out the door on his feet," Henderson said rather testily. "Where'd he come up to on the door?" Pierson stood by it and raised his hand slowly until Polski said, "That's about right."

"Close to your height then, close to six feet," Henderson said evenly. "Thank you."

"Can we have a look upstairs before we go?" Pierson asked. The chairmaker nodded, going back to his workbench. The two men climbed the stairs to what would have been the hayloft. There was nothing but the bare floor, no place to get a fingerprint, but Pierson dusted the railing—three years ago, what could it yield? No fingerprints had been found on the bomb fragments either. Polski was already working leather strips around the chair arm and seemed to have forgotten about the inspectors when they came down. He nodded as they said good-bye.

"The two visits of this Ozzie character fit into the time frame for two of the bombs," Henderson said, "but wait, we should get Polski's mug shot. Go back and ask if you can take his picture."

"I don't think that's a good idea. Look, if he's the bomber, we probably scared him off today. We have some time. Let's not show our hand until we're sure. Let me nose around some more with Betty Lou. Polski visits her on Mondays. Maybe I can catch him then."

"Well we don't have all day on this. Whoever he is, he may be planning a new incident. It would be helpful to show Polski's picture to the university people. They could nail it, give us a yes or no on the guy. Still, I can't believe he is the man we're looking for—he showed no surprise when you confronted him with the photos. I watched carefully. He's certainly into his chair-making. I don't know if he's also into bomb-making. Where would he keep his stuff?"

"I can't believe Polski is Ostro either, although he speaks a little high-falutin' for a chair maker," agreed Pierson. "Did you catch the 'this chap,' and the use of the word *abated*? The storm *abated*, that's pretty fancy language for a chairmaker, but not for a professor. Sam, I'd like to look into this guy's background a little further, even though it's a long shot."

"Good," said his boss. "I'll see what I can find on an 'Ozzie,' could be it's a version of Ostro. But get that picture. The college could identify him. And show his ears. Ears don't lie. I hate to think we'll be wasting time going on a wild goose chase for an itinerant 'snowman.'"

On Monday, concealed in the bushes around the side of Betty Lou's salon, Pierson took several shots of Polski entering the house by the residence door. He got a good profile shot with his ears showing, but the man had on a baseball cap and his face was partially obscured by the brim. He heard voices in the front of the house that was given over to the salon. Betty Lou was preparing to cut his hair. Polski took a seat in the salon's chair facing the window. She put a towel around his neck and turned to get her instruments.

Pierson laughed to himself. The guy has it made. He watched. Polski closed his eyes, head back. The inspector caught his full face through the glass.

Then he trekked over to the real estate office where the sale for the barn was handled. Perry November, round face, round belly, stripped shirt with suspenders, had made the sale.

"Well, he came in here, it's a while back now. Ah'd have to look it up, but he heard Ah had a property near the river and in the woods. Ah told him it was an old barn with no utilities. He said he didn't care. After we looked it over, he plunked down the full price. Ah think it was ten grand in cash. The money went to the heirs somewhere in Alabama. What's the problem, Inspector?"

"We're just trying to track a man who went missing several years ago and maybe doesn't want to be identified. I'd like a copy of Polski's signature if you can dredge it up."

"No problem," said November, puffing out his already puffed-out chest. "We keep scrupulous records. Let me put a search on it, can you come in say an hour or two?" Pierson touched his hat. "Much obliged."

He'd go to the cafe and call Henderson, tell him he'd gotten the picture. Henderson had news. A teamster at a truck stop said he had seen a man of Polski's description wandering between the parked rigs. The teamster asked the guy what he was looking for. He said he wanted the restaurant and that he thought he was taking a shortcut. The teamster told Henderson, "That seemed suspicious to me. I knew about the truck bombings, so I directed him, but I shadowed him. He made for the restaurant all right, went inside, but then when I looked around, I couldn't find him nowhere, not in the can or outback where there are some tables. Then I thought, I'm getting crazy. I have to be on my way. Didn't want to cause trouble for some innocent guy. Huh."

Henderson had the teamster's name and contacts. "We better brace for another trashing episode," Henderson warned. "Get back here as soon as you can."

When he returned to November's office, the realtor had the signature for him. The handwriting was bumpy, childish. "He wrote slowly," November said. "The scene just came back to me. Ah remember he had no interest in readin' the documents. Ah thought maybe he was illiterate." Or maybe trying to disguise regular handwriting, Pierson surmised. No matter, he'd fax the writing sample on to Dr. Mayfield at the college along with the pictures he had snapped.

November was still talking. "Ah asked Polski how he was gonna live in a barn when winter came. He said he'd insulate the barn and with the heat from his potbellied stove, he'd be okay. And Ah guess he is 'cause we've had some rough winters here and the summer can get hot too, but he's thrivin'—makin' his chairs and rakin' in the dough."

"Let me ask you something," said Pierson. "Does he ever leave his place?"

"Not that Ah know of. 'Course he does go off to collect wood. Betty Lou was lookin' for him when he didn't show up one Monday for their visits. Asked me if Ah'd seen him. Heh, heh. She found him comin' out of the woods. Said he was so late collectin' he just slept out there instead of goin' back in the dark."

"Do you remember when that was?"

"Hell, no," said November. "Ask Betty Lou."

"Could he walk to a bus stop from here?"

"Well, it's only two miles either way, in town or at a pickup point if someone's there to flag the bus down. The next stop is in Mays, about ten miles from here."

"So the bus stops several times before it gets to Asheville?"

"That's about right," said November.

"Is there a truck stop on the way?"

"Sure is," November said emphatically.

Pierson felt the ring closing around Polski. He could get from his place to Asheville and take the bus from there to any of the spots where the blasts had occurred. And going the other way, there were a series of small towns, one near a trashing. He could do his deed and get back the same day. But so could the other guy—Ozzie. On his motorbike he could go anywhere. Maybe, he mused, the trucker who followed him to the restaurant scared the trasher off this time. But if he were bent on the mission of destroying trailers, he wouldn't give up so without doing further damage.

Before he went to headquarters, Pierson stopped at a candle store in town. The people there never heard of a three-wick braided candle. In Ashville, the owner of a candle shop was also mystified. "I know what it is," volunteered a young, pretty customer with studs in her ears and one in a nostril. "It's a Havdalah candle. The kind you use on Saturday night in Jewish homes to mark the end of the Sabbath. You have to go to a Judaica store for that." The proprietor raised her eyebrows. "Where can I find one?" Pierson asked. The young woman directed him to a street some blocks away where a Chabad house had recently opened.

At the Judaica shop, Pierson showed his photos. The personnel were noncommittal, shrugging. "Did you see a biker come by to buy one of these?" Pierson asked pointing to a candle in a show case.

"A biker, no," said the young man with curls at his ears and a *yarmulka* on his head.

"Could I see your sales slips, it would have been last April or March?"

The salesman laughed. "I don't know if we have a sales book from last March. Heshy," he called, "do we have sales books from last March or April?"

A man answered from a loft above the main shop, "Yes we do. But it would take time for me to get that box. What do you need it for?"

"Never mind, get it out, okay?" He turned to Pierson. "Heshy is doing our books today. He can't stop for that right now. Come back in a day or so, okay, or I'll call you when we have it," he said, taking Pierson's card.

"Make it soon, today if possible. Time is of the essence here. I could order it done now, this minute, but I'll give you some time. Call me." Everything is a hassle, Pierson thought. I could stand here and wait, but what really will I find?

At headquarters, he sent off his pictures and the handwriting sample to Mayfield. He'd like to nail this down before a next episode. But it was not to be. After a raging spring storm, the bomber struck again. This time, a trucker was killed. It was June 2, 1996.

Chapter 20

That spring, when Mort was on call, they would spend a weekend day at his home. Lila admired Susan's choice in fabrics and furnishings although they were a little staid for her taste. The patterns and upholstered pieces were very traditional, covered in green and blue damask. The living room reminded her of a page in a high-end home design magazine of the 1960s. Susan's portrait was above the fireplace. Sitting on a chaise in a long dress, she appeared in the painting to be a serious-looking person with lips parted in a half-smile. Lila thought she would have liked her.

It was a pleasant, well-kept home. Flora must have recently dusted because several lampshades were askew, and pictures in the room slanted. Lila went about straightening them, feeling a little guilty that she was intruding on someone else's turf.

After some outdoor play on a cool day, the foursome usually sat in the pine-paneled den where there was a TV. The girls sprawled on the floor playing a board game. There Mort could respond quickly to a ringing phone. Lila listened as he gave instructions to medical personnel who called, or comforted a patient's family. He sounded so compassionate. No wonder he was revered by his patients.

One Sunday, the last weekend in May, he sped away to an emergency, leaving Lila with the girls. Lila entered the formal living room to look at more pictures on the end tables. Andrea followed her. She glanced at Lila looking at her mother's portrait.

"That was my mommy," she said, taking Lila's hand.

"I wish I had known her," Lila said. "She looks so lovely."

"I want you to be my mommy now," the child said.

Lila bent down and hugged Andrea. "Sweetheart, we're together as much as we can be. Your daddy wants the best for you, but we need time. Can you understand that, Andrea?"

"I guess."

"Then let's see your beautiful smile."

"Come *on*! Andrea, it's your turn," called Chloe from the den.

Andrea giggled, and Lila giggled back. They had had a private moment together.

Lila let herself imagine being Mort's wife, Andrea's mom, and having a dad for Chloe. It all seemed so right. She glanced around the living room again. She would like to update the chairs and sofa with modern fabrics. The dining room held a mahogany table polished to a shine. She noticed the seats on the velvet chairs showed signs of wear. She was sure Susan would have had them reupholstered by now. She had only been upstairs to Andrea's room during the day of the funeral, and it pained her to think of Mort and Susan's bedroom above where she was standing. Was it jealousy—for a dead woman? Lila berated herself, realizing marrying Mort was only a daydream. Suddenly, she was overwhelmed with regret. Forget me and Mort. What am I doing to this child? What if Mort rejects me when he learns my true story? This innocent, loving child will have a second loss. I must find a way to end this masquerade.

June can't come too soon when I face the panel of judges. Hearing the reassuring sound of Mort's car as he returned, her spirits lifted.

The next evening, Mort called and said he wanted to come over to speak to her. With Chloe asleep, Mort confronted Lila.

"This hotel stuff is okay, but I want a home with you, Lila. Please, I've talked to you about Susan. I know it's not because I am lonely without a wife, but because you are the love of my life. Your sweetness, your curiosity—when I look at your beautiful face, a warmth spreads over me. Everything sparkles. You are what makes me want to get up in the morning. I'm begging you to get on with the divorce. It's too long. If you need a better lawyer, I'll be glad to pay for one. Darling girl, I adore you. I want to be with you and Chloe night and day. We have to get things straightened out. This Bronstein fellow has got to be dealt with."

Lila listened to Mort's loving words, her heart pumping. Oh, to lose this man would be too much—her strivings, her duplicity to people who had embraced her without question, her giving up her own family, her friend Judith. To lose all she had gained, but it was an abyss into which she had to plunge. She could deceive this honorable man no longer.

"Mort," she said simply, "there is no Bronstein. I got the name—I don't know from where—on my bus ride to this town. I must have passed the department store, and it stuck. I am married to a man named Alton Ostro. He's Chloe's father. I ran away from him. He is a murderous person. I should not have married him, but I was impressed with his celebrity and that this important man wanted to marry me." She sighed and gave Mort the history of her sorry marriage and what she believed were his frightening intentions.

"I thought I could become his muse, give him a warm home to retreat to when the pressures of his quest were overwhelming, but he wasn't interested in me. He was obsessed with his theories, he never looked at Chloe, her smile left him uncomfortable. He couldn't tolerate her crying. He shouted at us, banging the table! I was terrified he would harm her.

"If I had told him I had survived the crash, would he have welcomed me back, been grateful for my escape and the baby's? He would not. It would just be another distraction from his work. I couldn't bear that look of disappointment cross his face when he heard the news that we had survived. He wished me to disappear, so I did."

"Oh, baby, what a time," Mort said, grasping her hands with his. "Well, I'll be with you now. We'll have a lawyer serve papers on him. I'll get on it right away. Lila, don't weep, this is wonderful. We'll have a life together—if you want me."

"There's nothing I want more," she said, blowing her nose. They both laughed. Lila didn't like playing the weepy girl; she felt she was strong and sure, that she had proved herself over the last nearly four years. But now everything was uncertain. Ostro would know she had survived. Mort would know she had lived a lie. She let herself weep.

From then on, Lila was in a state of nerves. The idea of dealing with Ostro was a nightmare to her. She woke up in a sweat during the nights that followed.

Mort had a report for her a few days later. His investigation, through a colleague at the university hospital, drew a blank. Professor Ostro had left the university four years ago, and nothing had been heard from him since. Letters from the administration to him had been returned to sender. But last year the police in North Carolina had been making inquiries. He asked for details. No one would tell me anything more.

Lila was woebegone. She hated to put Mort in the middle of finding this crazy man. He was determined, however; he planned to hire a tracer of lost persons. "We'll find him. This nonsense has got to end."

There was no trouble finding Alton Ostro after all. The next day his name was all over the television news, and so was Lila's photo.

Chapter 21

It was now the first week of June. A week earlier, Inspector Paul Pierson was rock certain that Jan Polski was indeed Alton Ostro. His photo, taken through the window of Betty Lou Brown's shop, had been confirmed by the university people. The handwriting sample had been pored over by a document examiner, who knowing nothing about the writer said this was an adult's handwriting, not a child's. "The person must be handicapped or is using a subdominant hand," was her conclusion. They should request that the subject write his name with each hand several times and then have her compare it to the sample that she had studied, to be certain.

Well, Polski wasn't handicapped; he wasn't illiterate either. He found out that Polski regularly stopped at the library on his weekly visits to town to borrow books and magazines. But, as his captain declared, "Okay, we know who he is, we know a possible motive, we just have to prove his connection with the bombings."

Pierson had not confronted Polski with the news that his identity had been blown. He hoped to nail the evidence of the crimes before that. Once the road had been cleared of debris following a spring storm that uprooted trees and tore the roof off several homes, Pierson sped to Polski's barn. The key was finding where he kept the supplies that would tie him to the crime. He had asked the chairmaker what he did to refrigerate his foodstuffs during the warm months. Polski removed a board in the garden. Under it was an insulated metal box set in the earth in which he could keep things fresh for days. Pierson was hunting for another such storage place.

The inspector had spent months looking for O or Ozzie and combed the Chabad sales book to find who had purchased a candle, to no avail. He asked for descriptions from teamsters at rest stops armed with Ostro's picture, but nothing concrete turned up. Pierson figured that the genius of Ostro, in his obsession to get big rigs off the road, led him to create this mythical figure in order to continue his vendetta against tractor-trailers. Now the wild goose chase was over. All he needed was the materiel.

Pierson was at Polski-Ostro's home site, tramping the woods, looking for signs of a buried cache. Polski wasn't around. Pierson heard his mobile ringing in the patrol car. He ran for it. Henderson shouted that the Trailer Trasher had struck again, and this time a man had been killed.

"Wait there for Polski—whatever his name is—and arrest him!" came the order. "We have police at the bus stop here, and I'm sending you backup."

Pierson was disheartened. The chairmaker had left his university, maybe because of his wife's death and that of the child. Started a new life but then twisted into this manic plan to get back at semis. This artistic man, so benign-seeming, was now a murderer.

Pierson was in the woods when he spotted Polski. He was disheveled, his clothing covered with leaves. It looked like he had slept on the ground. His face when he recognized Pierson was impassive.

"Put your hands behind your back, Mr. Ostro," Pierson said calmly. Alton offered no resistance. He was cuffed. Pierson said he had the right to remain silent. Silence, that was to be Alton Ostro's mantra in the coming months. Pierson was leading the man to his car when the police SWAT team arrived.

The headlines the next day heralded the arrest of the Trailer Trasher who had been dynamiting rigs in the Asheville area for the last three years. Pierson's photo showed the physicist, Alton Ostro, who had been hiding under the pseudonym of Jan Polski, a maker of chairs. The story explained that Ostro's motive for the alleged crime was the assumed death of his wife and daughter in a crash with a tractor trailer on the night of October 1, 1992. A picture of Lila Leif Ostro at her wedding was given prominence in the article; it had been flashed on the screen.

Pierson asked for Ostro's confession, but the man would not speak to him, or anyone.

"You're going to be charged with murder, Jan," Pierson said. Ostro hunched his shoulders and closed his eyes.

Chapter 22

Mort Shechter was making his rounds at the hospital when another doctor sidled up to him. "Isn't this your companion, Lila, the one whose husband has been arrested?"

"What are you talking about?" Mort shot back.

"Go look at the paper, Morty. It sure looks like your Lila," the colleague answered.

Lila was doing some paperwork in the classroom at the end of the school day while Chloe, waiting for her mother to finish, sat printing words in her notebook. Rabbi Gordon and the secretary walked in. "Chloe," he said. "Please go with Mrs. Green and help her for a minute. I have to talk to Mommy." He closed the classroom door. Lila's heart was pumping. What now?

"This is you, isn't it?" he said, pushing the newspaper toward her.

Lila's mouth fell open. There was the picture her brother Martin had taken at her wedding. She had never seen it. The black-and-white shot showed her holding the bouquet that Judith had given her. Her suit jacket was open, and Lila saw the *hamsa* dangling from the chain around her neck. In the photo her eyes were averted and her lips pursed. *I was looking for Alton,* Lila recalled bitterly, *but he had* walked away. And there was Alton's photo, looking older and heavier, sitting back in a barber's chair.

Lila read the story that described Ostro as a physicist posing as a chairmaker. He also had fathered a child with a woman from Perryville, the town where he had settled near Asheville.

So now it's happened, Lila realized. Face it. Say something.

"Oh, Rabbi, I'm so sorry I involved you and the community in this mess. I had no idea what happened to Alton, I just wanted to escape from him."

"I'm the only one who knows your maiden was Leif, so I know that you're the missing wife, although others may not. We will have to tell them."

"Of course, and, Rabbi, I'll resign immediately, or you can fire me. I don't want to cause you trouble or the temple—anything that will help avoid attention."

"Look, I know there must be more to this story, but my authority comes from the board. I'm going to have to consult them. And these people, they think you are dead?"

A rapid knock on the door startled them. The rabbi rose and opened it. Mort was standing there. He walked to Lila's side; seeing her beaten look, he grabbed her shoulder.

"Rabbi, I know about Lila, I stand by her in this mess."

"You knew about Lila's husband?"

"Not what he has done. I've been trying to find him to start divorce proceedings."

"I did not want to deceive you and Mort, Rabbi," Lila said. "At first, I thought I would just take some time to steady myself to confront Alton. But then, like a miracle, I found Ida, you, Rabbi, the temple, and Mort. It was heaven. I just wanted it to go on forever. Playing dead was my way of hiding from him. But no deception ever lasts, does it, Rabbi?" she said slowly.

"I've wondered about you, Lila," the rabbi said. "It says here you taught in the demonstration school at the university. I thought you were a remarkably able teacher for one with so little experience, as you led me to believe. Now I understand that you didn't want me to inquire at the university. They'd find out you survived. Pardon me for stepping out of my role, but this is really a soap opera."

Lila felt to hold back the final deception would be the worst lie of all. "There's more," she said, her voice barely audible. But then the determination to rid herself of that last misconception gave her courage. "I'm not a Jew," she said looking at Mort, whose face died.

The rabbi spoke. "In regard to employment at our school, that is not a consideration. However, the next step is letting the authorities know you exist. You realize that, of course."

"Right," Mort said without conviction. "She'll need a lawyer." The rabbi left them alone.

"Wow," Mort shook his head. "You do a good job of acting the part. Anything else in this quote soap opera I should know?"

"Oh, Mort, please forgive me. I didn't want to hurt you and Andrea. I've done a terrible thing to you both." She bent her head but kept herself from weeping. She didn't want to seem to be pleading for sympathy. She felt tarnished and shoddy before him. She looked up at Mort. "Now I must straighten things out for myself, Mort," she said evenly. "I thank you for coming. I just want you to know I love being Jewish. I don't expect anything more from you, though. You should not be involved in this. I'll manage. Now I have to get back to Chloe."

Mort cleared his throat. "I have a medical meeting in New York tomorrow. I'll be in touch." He turned his back and left the building.

They didn't have to wait long for the word to get out. The first one on the phone was a reporter from Philadelphia asking to speak to Lila Ostro. Ida, who was hovering over Lila, wanted to take the call, but Lila insisted.

"I'll speak to the reporter. Yes," she said. "Mrs. Ostro is alive. That's all we can say. Good-bye."

"Who's speaking, who is it?" called the voice on the phone, but Lila hung up.

"So now they know. I must call my brother, Martin. Oh, how I missed him."

Ida made this call. "I'm a friend of your sister Lila," she said. "Please sit down. I have some good news for you."

Martin was sobbing at the other end when he heard Lila's voice. His wife came to his side. "Lila is alive," he cried. "She survived the crash after all and was hiding from that bastard."

"I told you, I told you," a young voice said.

"Lila, dear, what you must have gone through. Brett thought he saw you at the holiday fair. I didn't believe him." He rubbed his son's head, then overcome, he let his wife finish the call.

"We'll come over if you like," she said.

"Ah, Cora, so good to hear your voice. Let's wait a bit. I have so much detritus to attend to. Speak to you soon, dear."

Martin was on the phone again. "Contact Raymond Gladding, in Cortland. He was a fraternity buddy of mine. He's a good lawyer."

"Martin, I can't stay here. Please find me a safe hideout."

Her next call was to Judith. Harvey answered. "I knew it! I knew it!" he screamed. "Even Judith said you were too agile to not escape. You'd not just sit there! But when we never heard from you—oh, we've been so sad all these years. Judy's out, but I'll call her on her cell!"

"I've missed you both," Lila said, her voice choking. "But don't call. It's too much for me. Everything is in chaos. Let me get things sorted out a bit. I'll call you again."

Lila contacted the lawyer in Cortland, Raymond Gladding. A wiry, energetic man, he was delighted with what he called his first interesting case. Lila had one stipulation. He was to answer all the questions that would arise for her. She was determined to keep herself and Chloe out of the spotlight.

Raymond was doing his job well. She and Chloe had moved to a motel that was closed due to repairs and only had a few rooms available to their regular tenants. Martin was able to secure a room for them. Raymond informed Ostro's court-appointed lawyer that Lila and Chloe had survived. His phone didn't stop. He was fielding calls and turning down requests for TV interviews. A swarm of TV trucks, cameras appeared outside his office. He waved them away, declaring that Mrs. Ostro was in seclusion.

Chapter 23

On a stormy morning two days after the news of Lila's identity made the headlines, a silver Mercedes pulled up to the curb on the main street of St. George. The driver exited the car and shook open a golf umbrella. An elderly man wearing a windbreaker emerged. Sheltered by the driver, he crossed the sidewalk and entered the doors of a glass-clad office building. Alfred Mandel, the former owner of a button factory, was not happy. He turned to the driver, "Twelve noon, Tony," he instructed the man. In the lobby, he met a fellow synagogue board member, Gus Gerber.

"Why pull us in on such a day?" Mandel asked.

"Well, Alfred, I mean this stuff is big news. Have you seen the headlines?"

"I've seen. It's a scandal. A woman takes advantage of our generosity, and we have the headlines."

"Well, let's see how we can handle it."

"I don't get you, Gus." They entered the elevator and exited on the fifth floor, the offices of Lawrence Mott, PA, Attorneys-at-Law.

The other members of the board were already in place in the conference room. There was a collection of newspapers on the polished walnut table. A gossip weekly shouted,

"Found Alive!" A local paper blared, "Teacher Hid Out at Temple Beth El!"

Alan Freed, the chairman of the board of their small synagogue, sat at one end of the table, Rabbi Gordon at the other. Freed, an athletic forty-year-old was rapping for order. "Ladies and gentlemen, please. Let's begin."

He was ignored.

"Did you know of this teacher's masquerade?" a man asked one of the women present.

"She is a lovely, capable teacher," said Sarah Bloom, who was on the school committee. "I didn't know anything about her personal life."

"Order please, ladies and gentlemen," Freed called. "We have other items on the agenda today, but we'll take this troubling one of Lila Bronstein first. I'll call upon Rabbi Gordon to give us some insight into the history of the young woman's deception here."

The rabbi turned from one member to another.

"I met Lila Bronstein at services in 1992," he said with quiet certainty. "She came with Ida Goldring, her landlady. I needed a teacher for the four-year-olds immediately, as you know." He nodded to Max Faber, the father of the then-pregnant Rachel, the teacher in the pre-K school who was ordered to bed rest. "Mrs. Bronstein had excellent credentials, and she has proved a fine teacher. The kids love her, the parents have nothing but praise for her. She's handled some difficult situations with a steady hand in the nearly four years she's been with us."

"That's all well and good, but these deceptions—she lied about her name and let people think she was dead! Doesn't she have family? Didn't anybody know? What kind of person is that?" challenged Larry Mott, the lawyer in whose conference room they were meeting. "It's a question of character here, Rabbi."

"I submit that there was a situation that you all have read about endlessly by now. I think her first consideration was protecting her child. She was living in fear and found a safe harbor in our community."

"Very nice, but with all due respect, Rabbi, maybe if you hadn't been so hasty hiring Mrs. Bronstein—or whatever her name is—this trouble could have been avoided," challenged Mott. "Didn't you check her credentials, a woman who just moved to town?"

"Let's not second-guess the rabbi," offered Clara Marcus, a stout woman, a former social worker. "He needed a teacher. Her circumstances were indeed unfortunate. But as the rabbi said, she does an excellent job with the children."

"We do not want our synagogue drawn into this media free-for-all. That's all I care about," added Gus Gerber.

"Then there's the question of religion," put in Max Faber, a longtime member of the board. "She has pretended to be a Jew, but she's not a Jew? Do I have that right?"

"Better than my grandson who has become a Buddhist!" grumbled Mandel.

"Marc still considers himself a Jew," the rabbi said softly, directing his gaze on Alfred Mendel, the well-to-do benefactor of the temple.

"All right," interrupted the president, "let's stay on topic, ladies and gentlemen. Rabbi, what does Lila Bronstein say for herself?"

"Very little. She feels she has betrayed our trust and has no right to defend herself. She, in fact, has resigned. It is up to you to accept her resignation or do otherwise."

"Well, I'd like to speak to her!" said Alfred Mendel, who knew his words carried weight with the other members. Several nodded in agreement.

"We don't want to be gossiping now," warned Freed, a graduate of the Institute of Religion who made a strict morality the core of his contribution to the board.

"It's not gossiping to interview the young woman," said Mendel rather testily. "She's been in our employ for over three years. She's influenced our children. What have these innocent children been learning from her, Rabbi?"

"Mrs. Bronstein—er, Ostro—follows our curriculum. I don't think she discussed her family problems with the four-year-olds," the rabbi replied with a half-smile.

"How will it play out if we accept her resignation? It will seem that we are convicting her of misdeeds," cautioned Gus Gerber. "We should give her a hearing."

"Hear, hear," called out the elderly Mandel.

"Very well, how many agree to interview the teacher?" Freed asked. Five hands went up.

"Your reasons?" He nodded to the stout former social worker whose hands remained down in her lap.

"I too am on the school committee, and I have observed Ms. Bronstein in the classroom several times. She is a most engaging teacher. She is preparing them for the demands of kindergarten. But there's another consideration, Dr. Shechter."

"What's that got to do with anything?" asked Mendel.

"Well, he's had enough trouble and this will only embarrass him further," the woman answered. "I feel this is a difficult time for Mrs. Bronstein, and she should not be disturbed. We know the story already. We should decide what to do right now."

"Thank you for your comments, Clara. Any other comment? The consensus is that we will ask her to appear before us," announced Freed. "Please make the arrangements, Rabbi. Now we'll turn to other business."

Chapter 24

A few mornings later, Raymond Gladding called Lila. "I've just heard from Ostro's lawyer, Mac Halloran. He wants Ostro to plead not guilty and to claim he had no motive to trash trailers as he knew that you survived all along."

"That's crazy, Raymond, he knew no such thing."

"Well, the lawyer says the insurance refused to pay on the policy you had on the car, and he never sued, as proof that he knew you survived. He never tried to pursue the trucking company either. And the police were uncertain. He said you were an athlete and able to exit the car in the moments it rested on the stump."

"Of course that is true. I did exit the car, so what? If he knew I was alive, how come he didn't contact me? I think he had repressed anger all his life, and this crash was his excuse to let it surface."

"Well, Lila, the attorney asks you to say you had contact with Ostro, so he could make that case."

"I'll do no such thing!"

"You know the penalty is severe for this man."

"Raymond, if you want to represent me, you'll have to understand I want no part in Ostro or his attorney."

"That's what I told the guy. My client wouldn't agree to that sham. But I had to ask you. He is Chloe's father, after all."

"Yes, that's hard. I'm trying to shield her, but she's already seen my picture and guessed that her father is accused of a crime. I had told her, when she asked about a daddy, that her father was an important professor but that he wanted his freedom, so we left. That child, she has his smarts though, I found her trying to sound out the words in the paper. Raymond, he wanted us gone, so why did he trash trailers? He should have rejoiced. His repressed anger found its out in this," she sighed. "Oh, God! When will it end?"

"There'll be a trial of course. I'm trying to keep you out of it."

"Thank you, Raymond."

"By the way, I examined the picture of the trailer and the man who had been killed. I noticed a tree limb next to his body. There had been a storm out there the night before. I told Ostro's lawyer to enhance the picture. It's possible the fallen limb killed the man, not Ostro's bomb, which was a distance from the man on the ground. And I mentioned that Ostro never attached his bombs to the cabs, only the rear of the trailers. I don't think he ever wanted to kill anyone."

"I hope that's true," said Lila, exhausted from the conversation. "Please suggest when it would be appropriate for me to file for a divorce?"

"Yes, ma'am," Raymond Gladding responded, signing off.

In a desperate attempt to give Chloe some sense of the normal, they exited the nearly deserted inn early in the morning and drove over to spend Sunday with Martin's family. Cora welcomed her, and Brett included his cousin in his early-morning Internet games, explaining the strategies to her. Sitting at the breakfast table, Martin smiled at Lila.

"A man has been calling here, twice since yesterday. He's a good friend of yours, he says. He wants to contact you. Listen, a lot of crazies get a number from the Internet. I put him off."

"You did right, Martin. No one knows where I am, even Mort, whom I love and probably have lost."

"Mort Shechter by any chance?"

"Yes," Lila said breathlessly.

"Well, that's the man. What shall I tell him?"

"Tell him I love him," Lila said, choking on her words. "No, no, no, don't say that. He may just want to be polite. Find out what he wants to say. That's all we can do."

Then Lila told her brother and Cora about the wonderful Mort, whose face had died when he found out she lied about being Jewish. "Actually, I never said I was a Jew. I just let people think that. I never corrected them. And this past Sunday, thank God, I was confirmed as a Jew, as you know."

"Right," her brother said.

When Lila had taken Chloe to the mikvah, the week before her deception was revealed, they were two giddy girls entering the indoor pool. First, though, they showered in the preparation room. They washed their hair and brushed their teeth. The mikvah lady examined their nails for cleanliness and then gave them each a towel. She looked away as they entered the small warm pool with its water running through it. She turned around once they were submerged and then instructed them to dunk their heads and completely submerge. Chloe held her nose and went under, laughing as she pulled her head out of the water.

"We can do that two more times," Lila said. "Are you ready?" The mikvah lady made sure they went completely under. Then she turned away so that they could climb out and return to dress in the preparation room. After, she signed a certificate that proclaimed that they had been to the mikvah and performed the required immersions. Lila said the blessing, thanking God for his commandments and the one for immersion.

With the revelation of her lies, the following days, she was in torment. Would the Beth Din accept such a person? Rabbi Newman called, not mentioning the news, to ask her to appear at the synagogue on Sunday at four in the afternoon.

"Rabbi, have you heard the reports about my deception?"

"Yes, daughter, and I have spoken at length with Rabbi Gordon. You've had quite a journey. We are scheduled to meet with you on Sunday. I can expect you and Chloe. Yes?" Lila was so choked with feeling she could hardly respond. "Yes," she whined.

Rabbi Newman had enlisted two learned men in his synagogue for the Beth Din. He had explained to them that Lila had taken the required course of study, had learned to read Hebrew, and was sincere in wanting to be Jewish. Her other problems were not an issue in this matter. They agreed to convene the "house of judgment" for late afternoon. Lila drove to the synagogue. The rabbi greeted her in the lobby of the synagogue. He asked her to settle Chloe in the library and then come to his study. Lila told Chloe it was important that she remain quiet but that she could look at the books while her mother visited with the rabbi.

Head up, she entered the study as one would a court where a judgment of life or death would be rendered. There sat the elderly rabbi at the head of the table flanked by two others—an even older gentlemen with a kindly face and a younger one with a black beard and a stern manner. Lila took a breath.

The three men questioned Lila's motives and her understanding of Jewish law and practice, history, and ritual. They asked for her to explain the concept of one God. One of the questioners wanted to know if she was converting because of a romantic relationship. She said she was choosing to be a Jew aside from any relationship she might have. If Mort was going to reject her, she had asked herself, did she really want to be Jewish? Her answer was yes. She felt so certain she wanted to be a part of this faith where she had experienced warmth and friendship. She told the men, "To have a faith, when I had none, will sustain me for whatever life offers. To belong to something so ancient and reasonable is my road to a life of meaning." She was excused and left the study.

The Beth Din met while she and Chloe waited in the library. Lila surmised they had plenty to talk about, with her notorious reputation. Every minute seemed too long, but it was barely a quarter of an hour when the rabbi came in smiling. They were approved! Chloe and Lila ran to shake his hand.

"I wish to suggest Hebrew names for each of you: Chava for little Chloe. It means Eve, Chloe, because you are a lovely maiden. And Miriam, for you, Lila, since you always wear her symbol, the *hamsa*. You are now Jews, equal to any others."

"But aren't I Jewish already?" the five-year-old asked.

"Yes, my darling," her mother said. "This will make it official."

The men came out and shook her hand and bent down to take Chloe's hand in theirs. The rabbi recited the *Shehecheyanu*, with Lila and the men joining in. Lila felt an immediate lift to her spirits. *At least I have accomplished* this, she thought, giving Chloe and me a lasting identity. Now it was off to Martin's for a triumphant barbecue dinner, and she was ready to down the mug of beer he always served with it.

Lila was using her maiden name again, shucking off Bronstein and Ostro. She told Raymond Gladding to hold off on divorce proceedings. She did not want to make it worse for Alton than it was already.

Martin set Lila up with a cell phone. He showed her how to work it and cautioned her to keep it charged. He gave Mort her cell phone number. She waited for his call.

"Hello," she said breathlessly when it rang.

"Lila?" It was a woman's voice. "This is Marla Shechter Moss, Mort's sister. I think we met the day of the funeral."

"Yes, Marla. What is it?"

"Well, Mort asked me to call. I know he cares about you, Lila, but he's having—how should I say it—a hard time with all the changes. He needs to step back just now."

"Marla, I don't want Mort involved in any of this. It's my problem. It shouldn't be his. He's been kind enough."

"He really feels bad about not standing by you. He's afraid it will just complicate matters for you. I don't know how to talk about this, really."

"It's okay, Marla. Tell him not to be concerned. I'm glad this is why you called. My first thought was that he was ill. Please tell him, I am fine. My brother is helping me. I have a lawyer, and I'll be all right. I understand how Mort feels. He's doing the right thing, absolutely."

"He said if you need help—you know, with the bills—we'll be happy to help out."

"No, no." Lila's voice got a little testy. "I can take care of myself and my child. I have always done so. There was never a question of money between us."

Was she trying to pay me off, Lila wondered in terror, or believing that I used Mort's money in the past?

Marla picked up on Lila's tone of voice. "I'm very sorry. I didn't mean to offend you. This is very difficult."

Lila softened. "I'm sure it is for you. But I'm glad you called rather than Mort. That would have been even more difficult. Marla, one thing—if she asks, please let Andrea know we miss her, and give her a kiss for me, okay?"

"Yes, Lila, I will do that. She does ask for you and Chloe, the poor child."

"Well, good-bye then."

"Goodbye," Marla choked out; she seemed to be having trouble speaking.

Lila put down the phone. Andrea is grieving, she cried to herself. How will I ever make it right for this child? It's not that she blamed Mort for forsaking her. She felt relieved actually. She could think now of herself and her needs and not worry about affecting Mort, bringing him unwanted notoriety. It was better this way. She would not let herself miss him. She had no time for that. She was due in North Carolina for a deposition.

Chapter 25

Mort

Mort was on the phone with his sister. "I have a favor to ask, Marla," he said slowly.

"Anything, dear," his sister, who was older than Mort, was troubled by the thwarted romance he had with the teacher.

"You know, Lila is in a lot of trouble because of her psycho husband."

"Did you know about him?" Marla asked.

"We were trying to find him when this story broke. Marla, Lila is not in her home, but I have a cell phone number for her. I really don't want to call—it's hard—I can't see her until this all is settled. It's too upsetting to me and to Andrea. I don't know how to talk to her about it right now. I'm asking you to call her for me, to express my regrets but to tell her I have to wait out the next chapter in this saga—or something like that. Can you do it for me?"

"I'll call her this evening. It'll be a pleasure," she said sarcastically.

"How did it go?" Mort asked later that night, his voice sharp.

"It was all right. I said what you had told me to," Marla answered, trying to keep her voice even. "She sent kisses to Andrea. She was sorry for disrupting your lives—that you should not be involved in her mess. I'd like to slap her face! Does she understand what she's done? The little one was crying. She's a terrible woman—be done with her!" Marla shouted, her voice rising.

"Look, I'm at fault too. I never really pressed her . . . What's all that shouting?"

"Lenny is yelling at me. You were always too trusting, Mort. Lenny wants the phone."

"Mort? Len. Don't let Marla get to you. She's upset for the child and you. Things will work out, Mort."

"Leonard, I know how Marla feels, and I have consoled Andrea. But things are untenable right now. My thoughts are with Lila, but it's too disruptive for us. When things calm down . . . Thank Marla for making that call. Bye for now, Len."

Mort sat in his den. Andrea was asleep. He had a moment to think about Lila. To miss her. I guess I was always too trusting, naive, maybe a fool, he told himself mournfully. I can't understand how she would not confide in me. I thought we were so close—even though I never really probed about her marriage. Maybe I didn't want to know. What's wrong with me? I am thorough questioning my patients. I just never felt that was my role with her.

Then he mused to himself, I must confess I was soothed to learn she never had loved Alton the way a woman should love a man, the way we loved each other. But to keep up the charade for so long, with me, it's just too hard to throw off. Not that I am going to let on to anyone how I feel. I'll agree she's been in a bind and cut off all conversation on that subject. And I'll focus on Andrea—it'll just be the two of us again, he sighed.

Morton Shechter had always been a giving kid. He shared candy bars; he let Marla pick the channels to watch on TV. He played touch football on a field near his house with the other boys, but he wouldn't go out for the team in high school. He was husky enough and strong enough, but he couldn't throw another player down. Although he was a good skater, he refused to be on the hockey team for the same reason. He shied away from roughhousing.

When he was fifteen, his father sent him to work in the clothing factory during the summer. He observed the hardworking women bent over their machines. He wheeled his bin along filled with the fabrics for them to work on. He tried to greet each one by name as he passed the goods to them. Some of them smiled and bantered with him, but others seemed too weary to bother. He felt love for these woman who helped him and his family live well. He told father how hard the woman worked. "They're well paid, Sonny," his father said.

One time, when he used the factory stairs to go from one floor to another, he found a man smoking in the stairway. Smoking was forbidden in the plant, a reason for instant dismissal. With all the loose fabric around, it was paramount to prevent fire. That had been drilled into him the first day on the job. The man, a carter, crushed out the cigarette and looked fearfully at the boy.

Mort was afraid too. What should he do? He should report the man; he just glared at him. The man raised his head and stared back, thrusting his chin forward as if to dare him. Mort blinked and went on his way, his heart beating fast.

He felt he should tell his supervisor or his father about the encounter. But he hated the role of a snitch. Maybe it was a one-time lapse. And he was afraid of the man. He wondered at the man's look. Could the man catch him alone and beat him? I am a coward, he accused himself. He spent a restless night worrying. He resolved to use the stairs every day, as a monitor. If he found the man again, no question, he would report it.

A week later, he saw the carter in the bin room.

"Hi ya, kid," the man said grinning. He took something out of his pocket. A package of gum. "See," he said. "I chew gum now. Have a stick."

"No thanks," Mort said. "But good. Gum is good."

A week later, the carter was caught smoking in the bin room. He was fired.

That summer, he knew he didn't want to work at the factory. He wanted to help the women in some way. He found his calling in lab class in biology. The intricate way the human body was constructed, the interplay of the body's systems and how they worked together fascinated him. It was such an unbelievable network. He wanted to know all he could about it—the muscles, the ducts, the heart, how they enabled a person to move, sleep, feel. He would study medicine.

Now he needed more than his work and his daughter; he needed Lila. He needed her strength and thoughtfulness. He longed to see her smile that lighted up his own face. But he also needed to heal. He'd just have to give it time and time for her to be finally free. I'll just have to wait.

Chapter 26

Rabbi Gordon notified the board that his colleague Rabbi Newman had called him to say that Lila Ostro had been confirmed as a Jew by his Beth Din that week. She had been studying to become a Jew for two years.

"So why didn't she go to *our* rabbi?" queried Gus Gerber on hearing the news. "Oh, I get it," he said, nodding.

"But why didn't she tell us her intention?" asked Alfred Mandel.

"She didn't want to use her conversion to excuse her masquerade. A good moral decision," declared Clara Marcus.

After an impassioned plea from Alan Freed that they stand by their employee without seeking to interview her, the board agreed unanimously. He so stated that in a press conference.

"Lila Leif has been an outstanding employee of our school and a faithful temple participant," he said. "We have granted her leave until her situation has cleared."

That seemed to be the end of the matter for the temple. It was no longer a source for news or gossip, which was Freed's fervent goal in making the announcement. Thankfully, Rachel, the original teacher, was able to take Lila's place.

Chapter 27

The Deposition

Raymond Gladding had tried to keep his client out of the proceedings, but her involvement was inevitable. The prosecuting attorney had not seen her name on the defense attorney's list of witnesses. She thought that the wife of the accused would want to testify in her husband's behalf. Since that was not the case, it meant she had good reasons, and she wanted to hear them. Lila was summoned to give a deposition with Raymond advising her. It meant two nights away from Chloe, who would have to sleep at Martin and Cora's house.

Dawn, Cora's oldest, was away at college. That left a bed available in the room she shared with Sara, Martin's seventeen-year-old. Sara objected. "I finally have the room to myself, and you want me to bunk in with a five-year-old. No way," she announced. When Lila and Chloe arrived, the house was in an uproar. Cora calling Sara selfish. Sara crying. Robert, Cora's son, broke the impasse. "Look, Brett can sleep with me." Martin's son Dan, a member of the National Guard, would be on bivouac, so the bed in their room was free. "Chloe can have Brett's room, okay, enough of this stuff. Hello, Aunt Lila."

Lila and Chloe stood there. "Sorry," Cora said. "You see sometimes our blended family has some issues."

Lila laughed. "Doesn't every family?" That broke the ice.

"Sara honey, go put Brett's linens on Dan's bed. We'll make up the room for Chloe later," Cora said firmly." Then turning to Lila, she winked. "Let's do coffee."

Chloe loved to visit with her older cousins. She ran up to Brett's room to help Sara, blissfully unaware of the earlier battle.

———

The deposition took place in the office of the prosecutor. Lila was asked how she met her husband, how long she had known him. What was their relationship? Raymond had counseled Lila that it was okay to say they had agreed the marriage was not working. Lila, while unwilling to testify on Alton's behalf, was nonetheless reluctant to condemn him. She didn't want her statement to be anything but neutral.

"Can you explain your not revealing for four years that you survived the crash, Mrs. Ostro?" A young woman assistant district attorney asked.

"Since we had agreed to split, I thought Dr. Ostro would welcome the news that we were no longer a factor in his life."

"Did you not consider that he would want his child to survive?"

"The professor was very involved in his work, he had little time for the child."

"How did you feel about that?"

"I felt that his work was important and he should be free to pursue it without the distractions of the child's needs and my own."

"What needs were that?" asked the prosecutor, sensing an opening.

"Just the ordinary things of everyday life."

"Such as . . . ?"

"Helping around the house, starting dinner. Things that would take him away from his work."

"Would that be a reason for disappearing? Letting him believe you had perished?"

"At the time, yes. We were estranged. What did it matter?"

"And now."

"And now I'm sorry I misinformed everyone, including some new friends I have made, and making my family so sad."

"The lack of Dr. Ostro's availability seems hardly severe enough for you to hide for four years. Did your husband threaten you in any way? Did he seem to you of a destructive nature?"

"No. He was supportive, giving me any monies I needed for the house and baby things. But he had a remoteness that left me feeling alone. And he confessed marriage was difficult for him because he was so preoccupied with his work."

Suddenly, the color drained from Lila's face. Her mouth fell open.

"Mrs. Ostro, are you all right?" The older woman asked, moving toward her. Lila nodded. She looked up.

"I realize now saying all this, how guilty *I* am. If I had not hidden my survival, Alton,"—Lila took a breath—"the man, would have had no reason to go after the trailers." Lila wrinkled her brow.

The prosecutors took quick looks at each other; they stepped aside and conferred in whispers. Lila sat quietly with her hands in her lap, thinking about what she had just done.

Now the older prosecutor addressed Lila. "Did you have any contact with your husband during these four years, Mrs. Ostro?"

"No, I did not." The two attorneys glanced at each other and nodded.

"Thank you, Mrs. Ostro. I may call you as a witness to that fact if the opposing attorney tries to maintain that you did have contact," the older woman announced. Lila stood, somewhat dazed. The three women shook hands; Lila was free to go.

She rushed home to her family, but her homecoming was clouded by what she had come to believe she must do. That evening she was on the phone with Raymond Gladding.

"How did it go, Lila?" he asked.

"Raymond, I want to testify for Alton, after all."

"What? Why the change of heart?"

"Because I realize that Alton would not have tried to destroy trailers if he knew I was alive. It was his thwarted valentine to me," she said grimly. "I realized the part I played when I was speaking to the prosecutors."

"Did you tell them that?" Gladding asked.

"I told them I felt guilty. I'm telling you that I should testify on Alton's behalf. It's only right."

"But then you would have to reveal how Alton threatened you, Lila. That won't go down well for him."

"No, I won't tell anyone that."

"Then you will seem like a feckless spoiled housewife who took such a serious step as keeping your survival secret because of petty reasons."

"So be it. That's what I want to do, Raymond. Tell Mr. Halloran to put me on the witness list."

"I don't advise it, Lila. With your permission, I'd like to speak to Martin."

"Leave that lunatic alone," was Martin's immediate response to Lila's intention. "Any normal man would have grieved, have given to charity in your name, not try to kill people! If you don't tell the whole truth, you leave yourself open to be thought of as a fool. And you are not foolish."

"But I am guilty of misleading that poor soul, Martin. In all fairness, I must testify for him. I won't be easy until I've done so."

Cora took the phone. "Lila dear, don't damage your whole life for this one gesture. It really won't matter to the judge or jury. You can't use explosives, no matter what your reason—that's it."

"You're right, Cora. It probably won't make a difference—except to me."

"Call that rabbi of yours," Martin interjected. "See what *he* would advise."

"I don't have to call him, Martin. I know what he would say."

Gladding gave up. He realized Lila was not to be moved. He instructed Halloran to put her on his witness list. Alton's lawyer was very pleased for his client and didn't hesitate to tell the prosecutor. The trial was set for late September. With her new course clear in her mind, Lila felt free to turn her attention to renting a real apartment and applying for a new job. She'd keep the nightmare of seeing Alton out of her mind with her many tasks that lay ahead.

Chapter 28

Starting Over

Lila realized she would have to start over in Cortland. Her lifeline would be Rabbi Newman's shul. This more traditional synagogue appealed to her in a different way than the Reform congregation that gave her a start. The service was more formal—there was more Hebrew employed, which was a challenge to her, but the congregation sang with gusto along with the cantor and she was beginning to join in. During the Saturday morning service when the Torah was taken from the ark and part of a chapter from it was read, she followed along in the large Bible, trying to match the Hebrew with the English words on the facing page. She read slowly, but she knew certain words by sight now, and they helped her find her place on the page. It was a hunt she enjoyed. The scripture stories were fascinating, and the commentary at the bottom of the page was helpful. She sat alone, toward the back, not wanting to push herself into the mix. She didn't remain for the Kiddush luncheon that followed services because she was afraid to.

The first time she entered the synagogue, she realized this had been the synagogue that Mort's family attended until his wife had urged him to join the Reform temple instead. A bronze plaque designated an ornate room the Shechter Social Hall. This was where the Kiddush luncheon was held. Perhaps Marla Shechter Moss was there. She would think Lila was haunting them. She picked up Chloe from the classroom where the children gathered, and headed for home. It was enough to have been in the lovely sanctuary with its stained-glass windows. The atmosphere of peace soothed her, and the chanting of the cantor was a solace to her hurting spirit. Services over, she scurried away.

Her round-robin friends called. She was still part of the group, they insisted. She was so pleased to hear from the women but declined to join them just yet.

Martin and his family were curious about Judaism; they knew very little about the faith and had many questions for her. What was this "Chanooka" all about? They talked about beliefs. Cora was a Lutheran and knew her Bible; they discussed common ideas and those that differed.

Lila changed the subject. She needed to find an apartment. Cora volunteered to go apartment hunting with her. Cortland was a larger town than St. George and had a plethora of places to choose from amid a building boom. She found a second-floor walk-up in a garden apartment that was child-friendly. The rent was double what she had been paying at Ida's, but Chloe deserved a room of her own. She explained to Ida that she would be leaving her.

"Have you seen Mort?" Ida asked.

"No, Ida. He should not be involved in this turmoil. He's had enough."

"He'll come around, you'll see," Ida said, shaking her head.

Ah, Lila thought, an old person's wishful thinking.

Ida kissed her and hoped everything would work out. Ida admitted that she wanted to sell the house and move to a retirement home. "I've enjoyed having you here, but I wouldn't want to get used to another person. It's too much for me, this house."

Lila helped her pack away some of her many *chachkas*, plates from different countries she had visited with her husband, clocks from every mantel, and pictures of her grandchildren at every age in order to make the living room more inviting to the strangers who would be looking. She cleaned her rooms thoroughly, taking down Chloe's drawings but leaving the throw pillows that had brightened the sofa. They enlisted the teenager next door to put the crib and high chair in the basement. Lila didn't need them anymore. Ida would find a home for them with a needy family.

Chloe had been in a private kindergarten in St. George. School was almost out, and Lila took the child to the local elementary school near their new apartment in Cortland to be registered for the first grade. She told Chloe they would be using the name Mommy was born with—Leif. The birth certificate she presented to the principal read Chloe Ostro.

The principal, a hearty, buxom woman, Mrs. McCracken, was taken aback. She asked for an explanation. "Are you related to the Trailer Trasher?" she asked after Chloe left the office for a tour with an assistant.

"Yes, I am. He is presently my husband. You understand that I prefer to use my maiden name. I would very much appreciate your allowing us to keep a low profile. This is a very difficult time."

"I can imagine. I was only making a joke when I asked. Now I recognize you. They thought you died—wasn't that the story?" The woman could hardly contain herself.

Lila smiled. "I am a teacher too, you know. We always run into strange situations that we must keep confidential."

"Of course. You'll be fine here. Chloe seems like a bright child."

"Mrs. McCracken, she reads well. She taught herself. You, of course, will decide what level she belongs in. I am very happy to work with you."

"We have a principal at Holly Middle, Martin Leif."

"He's my brother."

"A lovely man. Well, we'll enjoy having Chloe here. Let me show her the primers we use in our first grade, Ms. Leif."

"Wonderful," said Lila smiling. She knew this woman was bursting at the seams to tell the next person she met, "Guess who we have in our school!"

The assistant knocked. "Come in, please," the principal said. Chloe bounced in.

"Mom, they have their own library in this school. And you can take home a book every day—as long as you bring one back!" Chloe took her mother's hand. "It's a very big school. I like it though. Shall I go here in the fall?"

Lila glowed with pride at her daughter. She overhead the assistant telling Mrs. McCracken, "She reads like a third grader."

The principal turned to Lila. "Mrs.—Ms. Leif. At the start of school we test each child. We do have a track for fast learners, so don't worry. Chloe will be properly placed."

The women shook hands. Chloe thanked her guide, who seemed amazed by the child's poise. "A grand girl you've got there," she said. Lila smiled, feeling a rush of pleasure. This was Chloe's first adventure into the larger world, and she was a success. What mother wouldn't beam over that?

Lila's next step was to apply to the school board for a job. A nascent four-year program had begun at several elementary schools, not at Martin's or McCracken's. Now they were expanding to another school some distance away, but near enough for her to be able to meet Chloe's schedule. Her enthusiasm for the demonstration project impressed the principal of the host school. She was hired on a one-year contract.

"Our school has a good crop of students, but many of them have parents in low-income jobs," Principal Warren warned her. "The kids don't hear English spoken at home and will need a lot of encouragement. Are you prepared to teach in such a challenging setting?"

"I would find it most rewarding to help these children acquire a good foundation for learning. This was my goal in becoming a teacher," Lila said firmly. "My classrooms have never been just playgroups, there's learning going on in every activity. I would love a chance to work with you and these students." The principal, an older African-American man, stood and shook her hand.

"Your success will be very important to the movement to make pre-K universal throughout the system, Mrs. Leif. I'm counting on you and wish you good luck."

The responsibility of success might be daunting, but Lila felt she was up for it.

She wrote to Rabbi Gordon, thanking him and his board for their past kindness and their consideration for her in her present circumstances. She explained her change of residence made her decide to take a position in Cortland. Later, she spoke to the rabbi on the phone and said she would never forget how the temple took her in. She promised to visit with Chloe sometime soon.

Lila's salary wouldn't start until late August. The car repairs, the lawyer, and travel to North Carolina would nearly devour her meager savings.

There were many flea market trips for furniture over the summer until she had assembled table, chairs, headboard, a set for Chloe's room, and a desk. The two of them were scraping and painting, refurbishing the nicked and scarred pieces she had bought. She purchased new bed frames, mattresses and upholstered pieces on time. "I just can't buy used bedding or a sofa," she lamented to Cora. "I had to have new."

"You wouldn't believe it, but our furniture was new once," Cora laughed. "It's gotten good use. But now I'd like to freshen up. Our girls are starting to bring home young men. I'd like to have a nice home. Martin doesn't allow any expenses we don't have in hand, so I'm saving up. It'll take years," she laughed.

"Cora, you are a wonder. You've managed all these children, you have taken me and Chloe in. You've been the sister I never had."

"Well, you're pretty special too. I don't know why your guy is staying away."

"Mort, I have to put him out of my mind. Perhaps it was the one romance I was destined to have. If that's all there is, I'm satisfied. It was such a deep, rich time." She blinked. She didn't want to let herself become emotional.

"Nonsense," Cora said, grabbing Lila's hand. "I found your brother after my husband died. I loved him, and I love and adore Marty."

"Mort was my world. What can I say? He spoiled me for anyone else, but I betrayed him. He told me so much about himself, and I held back."

"But you did tell him about the accident before the arrest."

"Yes, thank God I did, so he wasn't blindsided or made a fool of when it came out in the papers. But I hadn't told him I was not born a Jew. I *felt* Jewish. I forgot I was still in the process of becoming one. When I told him, we were with the rabbi who had been so welcoming to me, given me the job, never asking personal questions about my marriage. As long I was a good teacher, he wasn't concerned. And everyone assumed I was Jewish—I never said I was—but I saw Mort's face fall when I blurted it out in front of him and Rabbi Gordon. It wasn't just the deception. I think he wanted to be close to someone who was a Jew from birth. He joked about it, but he gets a lot out of believing all Jews are linked by heritage to King David. Where do I fit in? The difference mattered to him."

Cora shrugged. "If I remember correctly, Ruth was a convert, and she was David's grandmother! Isn't that right?"

Lila laughed. "I never thought of that, Cora. She was a great-great grandma. But okay. Still, you know the song, 'Know when to walk away, and know when to run.' Well, Mort ran." When she heard that song at the diner on her way to a new life, she was running from Alton. Now she was singing it again, her voice breaking.

"You don't know what was in his mind, Lila."

"I do though. I know him," she said with a dead finality. "I'm sure he's found someone else by now." She thought back to Mimi, alone with two children. Maybe Mort and she had found each other. As much as she loved Mort, she hoped that Mimi, with her cheerful smile who hid her loneliness, would find someone. If it was Mort, she would cry but be consoled.

The trial was set for mid-September. Lila was not happy about that. Chloe would be in the first month of school, and her four-year-olds would be getting to know their teacher and her routines. Raymond explained his client's difficulties to Mac Halloran, who said not to worry. She could be up and back the same day.

But happily, July was free. She was determined to visit her father in Flint and to take Chloe with her. They had spoken on the phone several times and she wanted Chloe to meet her grandfather. The garage mechanic vetoed her using her car for the trip. "This heap will never make it," he said. "If you want to use it around town, it'll probably be okay. But you're taking a chance to go a distance."

Lila groaned. There was no way she could afford a new car, or even a good used one. "We'll take the bus," she told Chloe brightly. "It'll be fun. We'll pass different towns on the way and follow our progress on a map. And after we've visited with Grandpa and Doreen, his wife, I'm going to take you to Crossroads Village, a wonderful place. I went there when I was about your age."

Chloe was all excited about the trip, asking a million questions. Lila told herself, I'm not going to let my problems wear me down. We deserve a change of scenery and I must go to my father before I regret not having done so.

Doreen picked them up at the bus station and insisted that they stay with her, and though Lila protested, she secretly was grateful for the invitation. It would be so much better for Chloe to be in a real home, with the warmth of granddaughter and grandfather getting to know each other than in a motel. Her father was taking a nap, Doreen said as they entered the house. "Go right upstairs to your old room. I have it all set for you and Chloe."

Lila paused at the entrance. She hadn't been back since she graduated from college and that was nine years ago. "My old room," she said with affection as they placed their bags on the floor near the window. It was a nice comfy room where she snuggled into bed and read by the lamp next to the bed. Doreen had cleaned it thoroughly—she could tell by the shining mirror and clear windows—but it still had a musty smell of old rags. And indeed, the lampshade's inner covering was falling to pieces.

"It's nice, Mom," Chloe said. "Did Uncle Martin sleep in the other bed?"

"No, no. He had his own room. Sometimes a friend slept over, or a cousin from Iowa visited us, and then it was good to have the extra bed." Lila hardly remembered the cousin, an older woman who was her father's niece and came through on business now and then. "It's a pleasant house, and Doreen has kept it up. I must thank her. Now let's go down and meet your grandfather. I hear his voice."

Bill Leif had a decent pension, but health problems had plagued him in recent years. When he left the house, he took a small stroller with him, holding his oxygen tank. He had a pack that hung from his shoulder to walk around with at home. Lila explained this to Chloe so she wouldn't ask her inevitable questions.

Lila realized how her father had aged. His previous robust form had shrunken like a plump balloon losing air. His hair, white as a cloud, covered his head, and his blue eyes sparkled as he looked at her.

Chloe said, "Hello, Granddad." He smiled at her and removed his breathing clip to kiss her and Lila.

"Well, my girl is having quite a time, I'd say," he chuckled, as he embraced Lila. "We were told about your accident, and I made a call to the police for more information. There was a chap on the highway patrol that seemed skeptical, said he couldn't believe they couldn't find any traces of the victims. I said to Doreen, we'll hear from you yet. And here you are with a lovely lassie in tow!"

Doreen was making faces as if she'd like to question Lila but couldn't in front of the child. But Lila grinned at him, so happy to see his familiar face. A picture of Lila and her mother was on the fireplace mantle. "Grandmother looks like you, Mom. How old are you in this picture?"

Lila picked it up. "I think I was eight or nine. Yes, I'm wearing my hair short. So I'm nine. I cut it for gymnastics."

"Let's see your baby pictures," Chloe went on. "You were always beautiful, Mom," the child said, looking through a batch of photos in a box her grandfather brought over. I don't look like you, do I?"

Lila hugged Chloe. "You look like yourself, kiddo, that's a beauty of your own." Chloe was a plain-looking girl who resembled her father, but she had good features and her mother's bright smile. Lila felt she would become a handsome woman.

"See, this is your grandmother with your Uncle Martin." Chloe stared, bringing the picture closer. Perhaps she didn't realize these people were once her age. Lila wanted to take a few mementos home since she had nothing of her past to remember, so they made a selection.

After Chloe went up to bed one night, Lila asked her father why they had never observed any religion in the home.

"It's a lot of hooey," he said. "Never bought any of it! It's used to excuse senseless wars and persecutions. Have you seen how one sect tries to destroy another because of different petty rituals?"

"I've found, though, it's a great comfort belonging to a faith community. It gives you an anchor," Lila said slowly.

"Well, of course, you were adrift in another life with no family or friends, the church would hold some meaning for you."

"I didn't go to a church, Dad. I went to a synagogue. We're Jews now."

Doreen put her hand to her throat. Her father put up his hand toward his wife. It reminded Lila of Archie Bunker's "Stifle!" She controlled herself from laughing.

"If that's been a solace to you, I'm happy for you," her father said finally. "Judaism is the basis of other religions, why not go for the original," he chuckled.

"But you, Dad—have you not found the need to go over the words of the ancient believers as answers to even modern dilemmas?"

"Listen, I take joy in my surroundings. I look at the sky in wonder, in the budding of the flowers in May, in the vastness of our lake, and that's my solace. Of course, Doreen goes to church sometimes. That's okay. But it's not for me, and your mother agreed with me."

"I want to take Chloe to Crossroads Village tomorrow. Could you come with us?" Lila asked, "I remember having such a time there. I want Chloe to have the experience too."

"We'll go, okay, Doreen.?" Bill said. She begged off.

"I need a little time around here. Can you drive everybody? Your father has a new car, Lila," she said proudly.

"Yes, of course." She was glad her father would not have to glimpse her wreck of a car. Her family in Flint had a new one every other year.

Crossroads Village was like a yesteryear community. Artisans worked in little shops making brooms, grinding grains, pressing apples, and churning cream into butter. Children are allowed to help, and Chloe was completely absorbed in each process. She held her ears in the blacksmith's barn and grabbed her mother's hand at the sawmill. She declined to go on the carousel. "Too jangley," she said. Her granddad sat on a bench between their stops, and later, they all went to the café for lunch.

"This was a great day, Mom. Can we come back tomorrow?"

Lila shook her head. "Sorry, babe, we have to head home. Maybe we'll come up again next year, if all's well."

"Doreen is trying to get me to move to Florida," Bill Leif revealed.

"The warm weather would be nice for you in winter, Dad. You should consider it."

"Ya, but in the summer, it's hot as hell. Who needs it? And I can't own two places. At my age, you like to simplify. We'll see."

At their final evening together, Lila reminded her father of the present he sent for her marriage. "Thanks for sending me the silver, Dad. I have a lawyer, and he's trying to track it for me."

"I wish you luck. How did you hook up with that craz— oops. Why didn't you call me way back? We would have kept your secret."

"I was so caught up in my deception, I guess. I missed all of you terribly. If there's one thing good about Alton's apprehension, it is that it put an end to my charade."

"Is there anyone in your life? A pretty lass like you can't go to a nunnery. I guess they don't have them in Judaism," they both laughed.

"We have Dr. Mort," Chloe piped up. Lila felt the color rush to her face.

"'Nuff said," her father declared, smiling. "It was great that you both came. Perhaps we'll see you in Florida next year."

Back home in their garden complex, Lila set to work to add cheer to the apartment. It occurred to her that this was the first real home she had in which she could decorate as she wished. She never changed anything in Alton's rented dwelling. Her apartment in the old mansion was furnished. Now, poor as it was, it was hers to make homey. She thought lovingly of her mother, who liked plain fabrics and utilitarian furnishings—no such thing as a beanbag chair would ever find its way to the Leif household. But Lila saw one in a resale shop. She laughed as she brought it upstairs and plopped Chloe in it. At the farmer's market, she bought some plants for the table near the window in the living room and framed the pictures she had taken from the box in Flint to put on an end table. She found colorful placemats and a few straw baskets for decoration.

She could watch Chloe from the window, so she allowed her to go down to the play area. Chloe made a friend there whose name was Andrew Wong. He was a third grader in her new school. She found him sitting on a bench examining something in a jar. It was a cocoon, he explained. A silky mass was attached to a twig. The cover of the jar had holes in it. "I think this is a luna moth in the imago stage, I am waiting for it to emerge," he explained to her.

This was Chloe's kind of person. She could ask her millions of questions, and Andrew was eager to expand on everything he knew. Chloe wanted her own cocoon.

"We'll have to go look for one. Do you have a jar like this?" he asked.

"I could get one. Can we look now?"

"I'm not supposed to leave the play area," Andrew said. "I can only come here by myself if my mom can see me from the window." He pointed across the yard.

"Oh, me too. I forgot." She looked up at her window. Her mother waved to her. "I could go ask her if she will come with us to look."

"Not today," said the boy. "I have to go home in a half hour." He looked at his watch. Chloe asked to see his watch. She examined it and read the time.

They sat on the bench and talked about school until it was time for Andrew to go

"Will you come later? I want to see the luna moth," Chloe asked tentatively.

"Look out your window, if you see me, come down." He turned to go, then as if the rules of politeness he had been taught just kicked in, he said formally, "Very nice meeting you."

Chapter 29

The Trial

Alton's trial had begun. There was some reportage in the local paper. More on television. The gossipy news programs were intrigued by how the bomber had been hiding as a successful maker of willow chairs. It was reported that the price of his creations had skyrocketed. Three unsold chairs were bringing in thousands of dollars. He was no longer indigent, as he had claimed. There was a question about what became of the money he had earned during the four years. The court order came to open Ostro's bank account.

The manager mentioned Ostro's vault box. The material that Pierson was seeking to tie Ostro to the crimes was right there—magnets, wires, and a detonator. Ostro was guilty. Hard to believe the chairmaker was a physicist and a bomber. Had he hallucinated O in a manic daze? Was his lawyer going that route? The bank account was almost empty. But Alf Stoner had several thousand put away for him. Now that Ostro could afford to hire any lawyer, he was asked if he wanted to retain the one the court had appointed; he nodded.

It was established that Alton was Jan Polski. The handwriting expert had her three samples of writing with either hand and declared the document Alton signed when he bought the barn was written by the physicist. Dean Mayfield signed an affidavit, identifying his former professor. Pierson's vault find was dramatically exhibited. There was also no concrete evidence that Alton had known his wife and child had survived, so the motive of revenge on big rigs still seemed valid. The only course left to the defense was that O was still out there. But since there had been no further incidents, that seemed a remote defense too.

The major thrust of Mac Halloran's defense now lay on the actual death at the scene of the June explosion. Forensics determined that the victim, a driver, had been hit by a blunt object to the head. The fallen tree limb was the cause of death, not the explosion in the trailer further away from the body. After having successfully reduced the probability of a charge of murder, the defense began calling witnesses to Alton's precarious mental state and otherwise sterling character. Lila would be his final witness—a stunner that would gain sympathy for the accused.

Research done by a TV reporter into Lila's past revealed she had been what the reporter called a beauty queen. Lila cringed seeing Stephan's photo. He must be laughing, she thought ruefully. "King and Queen of the Prom," proclaimed the Flint paper from 1984. It was blown up on the front page of the daily. Lila and Chloe retreated once again to an unknown destination.

Raymond was successful in keeping the press at bay. "Although," he said, "if you want to make some money, the scandal sheets will be happy to pay for your story."

"Raymond, you know, I'd rather die first. I'm sorry, you would be compensated promptly if I did, but I will not."

"Look, I'm becoming a major voice here. That's good for me. Calls are coming in asking for my help in a bunch of matters. Also, I'm getting your insurance money for the car that was demolished in the trailer accident. It's not much, yours wasn't exactly a new car."

"I'm very grateful to you, Raymond. When will Halloran call me?"

"Halloran's defense is going well. The murder charge has been dropped. Next, he'll have character witnesses, you and Ms. Brown, and Ostro's students."

"I shall make myself as plain as possible, a nonentity."

"That'll be hard, Lila," he said admiringly.

At the other end of the phone, Lila couldn't help smiling.

Gladding called the next day. "You're on. Are you still determined to go?"

"Yes, Raymond. Dreading it but determined."

She drove to the airport and left her car in long-term parking. The early flight from Pittsburgh had her at the courthouse at noon. The judge had called a recess until 2:00 p.m. Lila had only black coffee on the plane. She had no appetite, and the thought of seeing Alton made her queasy. She realized she must fortify herself for the ordeal. She would try to get down toast with marmalade and black coffee. Wearing no makeup and a hat with the brim half-covering her eyes, she hoped to avoid attention.

As she brought her tray to the table, a sweet-faced buxom woman approached her.

"Lila?" the woman whispered. Lila looked at her in alarm.

"It's just me, Betty Lou Brown. Our daughters are half-sisters."

Lila's mouth fell open.

"Can we sit down?" Betty Lou asked.

"Of course, I'm sorry. I forgot about . . . Why are you here?"

"I'm a character witness for Jan, that is, Alton Ostro."

"Oh, Betty Lou, I am too. I feel so bad for him."

"Listen, that's not what Ah wanted to speak to you about before we have to be ready to go in. Ah wondered, wouldn't you like the girls to meet? My Mollie would love to know her sister. She's four and very bright."

Lila smiled. "Chloe is too. Alton's genes, I guess. But about meeting? Let me think. We live so far apart. And really, what do the girls have in common—that their father will be in jail?"

"I just thought—" Betty Lou stammered.

A young woman approached them at the table. It was the assistant prosecutor Lila had met on her last trip.

"Ladies, thank you for your help. You'll be happy to know that the case has been settled."

Betty Lou was the first to respond. "And?"

"Dr. Ostro pled guilty to a lesser charge. He will probably receive twenty years. Using explosives, as he did, is a very serious crime. Mrs. Ostro, Ms. Brown, your testimonies are not needed. You are free to go."

Lila nodded. She was overcome. She would not have to see Alton at the defense table, something she dreaded more than being on the stand.

The attorney left. Lila began hyperventilating, her chest heaving. "Poor Alton," she whispered between breaths. "The poor soul. He didn't know how to live, and now a prison. I feel so guilty. I should have done more." But then the vision of him at the crib with the pillow made her recoil.

Betty Lou held her arms. "Don't blame yourself. He had four productive years in his retreat. He took his rages out on those trucks, I guess. He loved living simply, and now he can be relieved of all the efforts to feed himself and keep himself warm. The dear old thing, he had no interest in Mollie, but he gave me a wonderful kid, and you too."

The two women held each other. "Thank heaven it's over." Lila squeezed her hands into her face. Then shaking free, she turned to Betty Lou. "Is there anything we can do for him?" she asked.

"I will visit him as soon as I can," Betty Lou said. Lila's blood stopped.

"I could not do that, Betty Lou, but if you find he needs something, here's my address. Let me know so I can send it to you." She scribbled her phone and address on an envelope. "I think my attorney can also find out for me. I'll be filing for a divorce. We didn't want to harm him by asking for it during his ordeal."

"I understand," Betty Lou crooned. She seemed totally sympathetic to Lila. Later, Lila thought, What a nice woman. Now her desire was to escape reporters. She sought a way out of the courthouse to a cab that would avoid the crowds.

"I'll go out front," Betty Lou volunteered. "Let them question me."

"You are a dear," Lila smiled at her. They found a guard, asking him to show her a private exit and call on his phone for a taxi to the airport. She hugged Betty Lou and thanked her once more.

The older woman searched Lila's face to see if she could approach her again about the girls; she had brought a picture along to show Lila should they meet. But long years dealing with her customers in the beauty salon taught her when to ask and when to shut up. This was a time to say good-bye.

Chapter 30

The Avenger

Alton left the university town in 1992 with a stack of hundreds from his bank account and a gym bag with essentials. He went to the bus station and boarded a southbound bus. *Too cold here*, he mused. Some place warm, with scenery, mountains, and woods. At the Port Authority Bus Station in New York City, he bought a one-way ticket.

North Carolina, far away, a small city, Asheville. That sounded good to him. Take another name so the people he left behind couldn't find him. Polski, next-door neighbors to his grandparents, probably dead by now. John? No, not ethnic enough—Jan. He warmed to the idea as the bus sped along.

I'll work with my hands. That's what I want to do. Let my brain rest. It's driving me crazy. He stared out the window of the southbound bus. Here's a town, small, looks like it would have a hardware store where I can get supplies. I see a school, a library, a supermarket. Okay, this is it, Perryville. Who ever heard of Perryville? "Getting off here, driver."

He bought the place that bordered the stream. Axelrod, the hardware-store man, said it would take a week to assemble what he needed—the lumber cut to size, the insulation, the iron potbelly stove, the chemical toilet. Fine, I'll stay in Ashville for the week, he thought. I'll make a plan.

He found a motel. His room faced a sea of rigs with metal trailers parked for the night. Those are the monsters that killed her, he realized. He stared through the window with rage boiling up inside him. "I'd like to demolish all of you!" he grunted through his clenched jaw. Why not, he thought. Find a way to gut them. Blow 'em up.

Get supplies while you're here, where no one knows you. A big town, you can go from store to store to build your stock. Some magnets. They sell fireworks here? Find out. You can use the powder to make a bomb. Get some pipe. Fuses. Plan, plan. You can do it. You will do it!

Alton hopped from one merchant to another, purchasing a few strong magnets in each store. He took a bus over the state line to Tennessee where he bought a basketful of fireworks. In his motel room, he removed the powder from each explosive, filling a large jar with the black stuff. He tossed the trappings into a garbage bin.

Back in Perryville, he opened a saving account in the local bank and rented a large safe-deposit box. He bought a satchel where he stowed his supplies and placed the bag in the bank vault.

When he returned to the barn, he saw that Axelrod had delivered the materials and supplies as promised. He went to work insulating the area where he would sleep. He had bought an iron bed and a new mattress and some flannel sheets, a pillow and two Canadian blankets. He put up a shelf for a cup, two sturdy plastic plates, two bowls, and two large glasses. Under the shelf he placed a strip of wood with hooks from which he hung two pots, a large spoon, and a broad spatula for turning fish that he expected to catch in the stream on the edge of his property. Axelrod had filled his order for tools. He would make his own table and chair and a bench or two.

He spread the flannel sheets on his new mattress and fell asleep. He woke at dawn ready to work. In a week he had insulated the section of the barn under the loft above. He had made the base of the table from the two-by-fours and laid a plywood sheet on top. He cut a large log he found in his woods for a stool and began work on a chair using branches that he scavenged in the woods that surrounded his homestead. He bought a wagon in town with big rubber wheels, put stakes around it to hold large items securely. He stocked it with beans, rice, canned fish, tea, oatmeal, apples, and oranges. He did not expect to go to town again until he was out of food or ready to execute his grand plan.

He worked on his chair. He experimented with twisting the green branches with lengths of larger branches. He realized he would need leather strips to bind them, but in this first attempt, he bored holes in the larger branches and forced the smaller ones into the holes. Glue would make the bind even stronger. He'd have to get cured leather strips and wood glue. He sat in his chair to see if it would hold him. It wobbled. He went to town dragging his wagon, a two-mile walk. Axelrod sold him the glue and directed him to a mountain outfitter near the entrance to the Appalachian Trail in town. There he was able to purchase the leather strips. After he made the chair sturdy, he decided to try a rocker. He used vises that Axelrod supplied to fashion his long branches into curves. Some he made into short circles to become the arms of the chair. He had to hew the wood to make the rockers and for the seat. It was a painstakingly slow job to get the shapes right without power tools to help him. He sanded the seat he fashioned, attached the rockers, and with glue and leather to bind the pieces together, he had a sturdy rocker. He sat on his stool at his worktable and thought about his plan.

He would take precautions so that nothing could be traced to Jan Polski. He would walk eight miles to the bus stop outside of Mays, wear a baseball cap and a long dark sweater, his jeans, and sneakers. He'd board the bus for Asheville and scan the highway for a trailer stop. When he spotted one, he'd get off at the next stop and walk back. If he started walking before dawn, he could execute his plan and return on the late bus to Mays. He had a canvas log holder in his satchel. He'd load it with branches and walk home. If anyone saw him, he was out collecting.

He made a trial run just to see if all this was possible. He spotted a motel where they allowed semi drivers to park their rigs in the back lot near the woods. That was a perfect spot.

Now he just had to make his bomb and test that. He got his box out of the vault and wheeled it home covered with groceries. He took out a length of pipe and cut off a ten-inch section. He crimped one end in the vise. He poured the black powder into the pipe, inserted a length of rope that was to be the fuse, and crimped the other end.

He went to the edge of his property, placed the bomb in the scrub there, and lit the fuse. He stood away to watch. The fire reached the bomb and stopped. Nothing happened. The fire never reached the explosives. He'd have to refine his method. He opened one end of the pipe and hammered a small hole in the metal. He inserted a new length of fuse, lit it, and stepped away. The pipe popped; metal fragments were flung in the air. But the explosion would hardly make a dent in the undercarriage of a trailer. He'd have to make his product more powerful. It would take a larger pipe, more black powder, a longer fuse so he could be clear of the explosion. He fashioned his bomb with care and placed it in the satchel in the hayloft that covered part of his barn. He trundled his remaining supplies back to his vault under a chair that the merchant had bought from him. By spring he was ready to act on his plan.

His life as Jan Polski was going well. A woman in town accepted him into her home each Monday where he showered and let her seduce him. He ate a hearty dinner at her house or else they went to the café on the main street where he had the turkey dinner special, heaping his plate with sliced meat, gravy, and mashed potatoes. People stopped by to chat with the hairdresser. He was a shy, quiet person in this friendly town. The woman got him a customer for his chairs, and he kept himself busy fashioning branches and creating chairs, a table now and then. He now bought the seats and rockers from a lumber yard so he could work faster. In town he was Jan the pleasant chairmaker. When he thought about his plan at home, he was Alton the Avenger. He was ready.

Alton walked to Mays where no one knew him—eight miles carrying his satchel. He boarded the bus and went another twenty miles to the stop past the motel that was his destination. He walked back. It was early evening. The place was quiet; the drivers sleeping or at dinner. Two trailers, parked nose out, the trailers against the woods. He cowered before the tin monsters. They seemed to him like two whales, glittering menaces in the waters around them. One of those leviathans, on a dark night, had breached, heaving its huge body toward an innocent speck in the sea, wreaking havoc on her, his small creature. She was dead to him, and the leviathans had been the reason for his loss.

Excitement stiffened his fingers as he approached the silver monster. He opened and closed his hands to bring them to life. Now nimble, he attached his device with the magnet under the whale's hulk. No one was near. He lit the fuse and disappeared into the woods. Some distance away, he heard the boom. A warmth flooded him. He had done it, a small first retribution for the damage that had been done him

He walked to a factory further on where the day shift was leaving and the swing shift taking its place. He caught the bus with the workers and exited at Mays. The eight-mile trudge to his homestead didn't faze him. He was energized by what he had accomplished. He gathered fallen branches in the log carrier. He sat down to rest on the river bank that bordered his property. He fell asleep. When he woke it was dawn. He staggered home with his load of branches, certain that no one was around to see him, disheveled, dirty, but inwardly at peace.

Now the trial was over. A new phase in his life would begin. Alton gave Halloran a weak hand when the verdict was read. The lawyer was very pleased with himself. What started as a murder trial ended in a plea deal that might get his client released in fewer than twenty years. "I must tell you, Alton, that the fact that your wife was on the defense list had a lot to do with our deal in your favor."

"My wife?" Alton said, dazed. He seemed not to comprehend. All he knew was that the handcuffs had been reapplied and they were leading him away.

Chapter 31

Lila, more than anything, wanted privacy. Her flight back would give her a little respite now that the ordeal was over. She slumped in her seat in the plane. She felt depleted. The curtain on the soap opera had finally rung down.

Judith, with whom she had spoken weekly, invited her and Chloe for Hanukkah. Lila put her off. She didn't have the money to make the trip. She owed on the furniture; she owed Raymond, and the car needed expensive repairs. For the first time, she realized how hard it was to be on her own. She considered taking a weekend job, but she didn't want to fall back on the kindness of Cora to watch Chloe. Finally, during Christmas, she found a temporary sales job at the mall. She insisted on paying Mrs. Wong, who had agreed to take care of Chloe during the holiday. Andrew was fine with that as Chloe liked anything he liked—museums, visits to the library, walks in the forest if it wasn't snowing, watching the Discovery Channel on TV. Mrs. Wong, a diminutive figure in a black snowsuit, went patiently along with these two studious children.

After the holiday ended, Lila was added to the sales force on Saturdays. The boost in her earnings helped her pay off the bills on the furniture. Her car was fixed. Raymond she would be paying for several years.

Her work in the public school was a challenge. She realized she had only taught in elite institutions with children from privileged homes. Now she faced a little United Nations each day. Many came from homes where English wasn't spoken. She knew how she tussled with Hebrew and understood how amazing her kids were picking up English on the playground and hopefully in her class. Nearly all were enrolled in the breakfast program. Some children came to school clearly ill. Almost daily she had to send a student to the nurse's office. The four-year-old remained there throughout the session because there was no one was able to come to pick up the child.

Lila requested an aide who spoke Spanish and one who spoke Creole to help her. There were no funds available for that service. She asked a mother to stay for a few minutes to help convey fire drill instructions so they wouldn't be frightened during a test drill that was scheduled that morning.

Her students were anxious to hear the stories Lila read and to do the projects at the tables. She relied on a lot of repetition. "Mata, please take a blue crayon. Maria, please take a red crayon. Angel, please take a yellow crayon," she'd say when handing them out. She employed a range of words about their paintings. "Those are lively colors you used today, Tiffany." To another child she said, "You worked hard to create that picture, Alonzo. You made four windows in your house."

Otto used his paints to cover a sheet entirely in brown. Another student called it a dumb painting. Lila asked Otto to explain how he got the brown color. He shrugged at first, and then he said, "I put all the colors on and rubbed them with my brush and they turned brown."

"Otto was experimenting. Now he knows how to make brown," she told the others. It made her think of the color field paintings of Mark Rothko and that gave her an idea.

She brought in pictures of famous paintings by painters who used different styles: the pointillist Seurat, the drip painter Pollack, and Stella, painter of stripes, and Rothko with his color field work. She asked the students to paint using one of these styles. Wild-striped pictures were created. Tiffany made a face of dots, including the outline. The favorite exercise, of course, was drip paintings. Lila unrolled a vast sheet of wrapping paper, and the kids, wearing their smocks, lavishly dripped colors from loaded brushes on the sheet until it was crowded with color going every which way. Then she made a banner, We Learned about Artists.

The children laboriously wrote their names on their works of art, including Otto, who was given white paint for the task. The display, including the blowups of the famous artists' paintings, was put up on the corridor wall. It received good reviews, including praise from the Dr. Warren, the principal who went around with the children.

"What made you do the dots?" he asked Tiffany, whose name was on a very neat picture of a face that looked like it had the measles.

"That's my Seurat," she declared.

Dr. Warren raised his eyebrows and nodded. "Very impressive," he said.

Lila was as proud of their work as the curator in a great museum of the paintings on her wall.

Lila taught the children by giving them real-life experiences. They made instant pudding, measuring the ingredients, pouring the mixture into paper cups. She brought in empty boxes of cereal, egg crates, and laundry soaps to make a grocery store to supplement the play area.

The children loved the store and learned the words for each item. They picked out alphabet letters from the familiar boxes they knew. "Brillo," the children called.

"Who can find the *B*?" their teacher asked. "Good, Carmelo. Now who can spot an *r*?" And so it went.

She was on her feet inventing every minute of the four hours of classroom time. The art project worked out well, but sometimes, she was so discouraged at her inability to move some children forward that she felt her confidence slipping away. Then, as if by magic, these children began responding in ways she had not expected, and her spirits lifted.

After the young students left for the afternoon, Lila straightened up for the next day's onslaught, wiping down the tables, putting every crayon in its slot, shaking out the mats, and putting the books in order. She mounted museum pictures of dinosaurs for the next day's class. She had a few minutes to sit down and enjoy the orderly classroom until it was time to pick up Chloe.

But life was a struggle. Without the leisure of Saturdays to herself and her daughter, she felt she was just a robot who had to keep moving, doing what she was destined to do without the joy of an adult to share her life.

She looked in the mirror one morning and, bringing her face closer to the glass, saw circles under her eyes and lines fanning out at the corners.

She told herself, what did I expect? Stress is wearing me down. For a person who likes things orderly, I've certainly made a mess for everybody. Then she brushed her hair, pinched her cheeks, and straightened her shoulders. "Carry on, Lila," she said aloud, followed by a morbid chuckle.

Her respite came on a Sunday in October when it was time for Chloe to attend religious school at the temple while Lila would go to the discussion group Rabbi Newman led.

As they approached the synagogue, Chloe shouted, "Mom, this is *not* the place! I don't want to go here. I want to go to the other place, where Andrea is and my friends are."

Lila parked the car. She faced the angry child.

"Chloe dear, we live in a different town now. You've been here before. This is our temple."

"Not going! Mom, why did we move here anyway? Where is Dr. Mort, where is Andrea?"

"They are fine, Chloe, it's just that we can't be together now," Lila said, looking at her daughter with compassion. "Of course you miss them. But we must wait until things clear up for us to be together."

"What has to clear up? Do they have the measles?"

"No, my darling, it's a big person's problem that we have to solve. It will take some time, but I hope that one day soon you will see your friend again."

"But I don't want to go to this place."

"Chloe, the school is expecting you. Mommy's going to stay and go to a class herself. It'll be good. You can hear wonderful stories and learn about the holidays. Besides, the boxes of cereal and crackers we brought for the food pantry are needed by people that don't have enough money for food. We must put the supplies in the box for them." Lila saw Chloe hesitate.

"Come, Chloe, take the cracker box, and I'll take the cereal, and let's go!" The child looked at her with pursed lips, but she exited the car, and the two made their way through the temple doors.

Lila sat in the class, but her mind was elsewhere. Chloe had always been so easy, but now Lila realized that the changes forced upon her had troubled the child as well as herself. Then she took comfort from Chloe's "revolt." Her daughter was able to express her feelings. She would encourage Chloe to share her thoughts in the future, no matter how painful. Bottled up feelings are what led to Alton's dysfunction. This would not happen to her child.

"Well, how was it?" Lila asked as she embraced Chloe coming out of class.

"It was all right. Some of the kids are going to my first-grade class at regular school. That girl over there, Tali, wants to arrange a playdate with me." The kids waved at each other.

"That's great!"

"How was your class, Mom?"

"It was fine. And I was asked to join a book club."

After the discussion group ended, one of the mothers approached Lila about joining. They met in the evenings in each other's homes and discussed the book they had read that month. Lila liked the idea but was fearful. What if Marla was in the club? She couldn't ask, but her new friend, Hindi, said the women were all young working mothers. That let Marla out. She was older than Mort, and her children were grown. And anyway, Lila told herself, I pay my dues here. Why should I be embarrassed? It's been five months since I last spoke to her. I am equal to any other congregant. If I meet her on a Friday night, I'll just say "Shabbat shalom."

She agreed to join the club. The camaraderie with other women would help. The next book was *The Man in the White Sharkskin Suit*. This was about an Egyptian Jew who was riding high in his world when suddenly everything was taken away from him. Well, she could identify with this man.

You have to endure, she scolded herself, although she smirked at the thought. I'm enduring. What else can I do? She thought about Mort every day and put herself to sleep reliving their tender moments.

She pondered calling him. Tell him the trial is over and now I'm free. The divorce papers are finally signed. Find out why five months have gone by without a word. I guess he was tired of asking me about the divorce, always to be put off. Maybe if I tell him? The idea was upsetting to her. She had to be realistic. He would have had to make his peace with her past, or if he could not, he would let her know that. He was too kind to keep her in limbo. Or maybe make Marla call. She grimaced at that unhappy thought. True, she had wronged him, but she had forgiven herself for the lie she lived in her desperate time. Why couldn't her beloved also forgive? The loss of her stolen paradise made her sigh at night. Call him? No, she mustn't force the issue; it had to come from him. She'd just have to wait as her crow's feet spread around the eyes he said he loved to look into.

It was not that she didn't have a man interested in her. The owner of the dress shop where she worked had asked her to have supper with him several times, but she made excuses not to. She could not look at another man—it made her feel unfaithful to Mort—yet her feeling of abandonment was like a lead weight pulling her down.

She so yearned to belong to him. She had never really belonged to anyone. To Gary, she was just a temporary fling. To Alton, she was at the bottom of his priorities. But with Mort, she felt whole, loved. *Ah-h. Don't start,* she told herself, as she climbed into bed after a long day.

Ida Goldring and Lila had been exchanging phone calls over the past months. It always helped Lila to speak to Ida, who was so accepting of life; she was a role model for Lila. This week, it was Lila's turn to call. Ida didn't answer. She hardly ever went out after nightfall, and Lila was determined to call the next day. The brittle tones of the recorded announcement said that the phone had been disconnected. Lila was alarmed. The following morning, on her break from class, she called Scott Goldring at his place of business.

"So glad to hear from you, Lila," he intoned with his cheerful voice. "Not to worry. My aunt sold the house, and there was an opening in the House of David, so she jumped on it. I know she'd be delighted if you would visit her there."

"I'm so relieved, Scott. Certainly I'll visit her. I'll call this evening when I'm free." After a few more pleasantries, they hung up.

Sunday, after Chloe's school let out, they drove to Ida's new home in the retirement community sponsored by the fraternal organization that erected housing for the elderly. It was situated between Cortland and Pittsburgh in a tan brick high-rise.

They were directed to Ida's suite, a large room with a sleeping alcove. Several of her *chachkas* were on a bookshelf with her children's and grandchildren's photos. Her visitors commented on the view of the meadow from her window. Lila brought Ida an orchid plant and Chloe one of her drawings of the Jerusalem hills with the Hebrew for Yerushalyim under the sketch. Ida embraced them both and set her presents down on her bureau. She invited them to the entertainment of the afternoon. They chatted for moments, and then Ida interrupted, "It's time to go to the assembly room."

The High-Steppers, a volunteer group of women from a nearby community, would be performing. Lila and Chloe trailed Ida to a large room studded with people in wheelchairs and walkers stacked on the side. Chloe was all eyes as more women and men made their laborious way with walkers and canes to the seats. Lila had explained to the girl that this was a place for the elderly who found it hard to live alone any longer. The lights went down in the room, and the stage lights went up as ten no longer young women, clad in red, white, and blue outfits with straw hats on their heads, came bouncing in to strains of "New York, New York." The audience erupted in applause. "Aren't they grand!" the women behind them chorused. Ida looked around to see if Chloe was enjoying the performance. The child was wide-eyed. When the dancers did the Rockettes' routine, raising their legs in unison, the audience cheered. She clapped along with the others as the troupe exited.

Then Ida invited them to go to the ice cream parlor on the ground floor for a treat. While Chloe licked a cone covered with sprinkles and talked with another little girl in the shop, Ida and Lila had a chance to chat. She knew Ida would tell her if Mort was engaged to someone, but she held back from asking about him.

"I don't like to pry," Ida said, "but how is the divorce coming from that poor man?"

"My divorce is final, thankfully," Lila responded. "Alton has been very cooperative. He seems to be holding up. I do get reports about him from my lawyer and the woman who visits him. Thank you for asking, Ida."

Lila asked how Ida was adjusting to her new surroundings. "Not bad," she said. "My son is coming to visit me next week from California, and that will be so nice. I know quite a few people here. We play scrabble and gin. The food is good too." She pushed aside the sleeve of her silk shirt and squinted at her watch. "It's almost time to prepare for supper," she said. "Here you are on a schedule. I'm so glad you and Chloe came, and I hope you'll come soon again."

With hugs all around, they left the facility holding hands. "Mom," Chloe asked, "those singing and dancing ladies weren't too good, were they? They couldn't get their legs up high or together. I wanted to laugh, but I knew that wasn't right to do."

"You were good, Chloe. You noticed how the residents enjoyed the performance, and those older ladies loved performing. That's what counted today." Then they exchanged glances and both broke out laughing, covering their faces. Lila made a mental note to call and see how Ida's visit went with her son.

On the Friday night, after their visit, when there was a Junior Congregation to go to, Lila came to the synagogue for services. She took Chloe to the small chapel where the religious school kids met, and went into the main sanctuary.

Although tired from a week of classroom struggles, she thought that the Friday service, with its soaring music and singing, would lift her spirits. How wonderful that the ancients conceived of a day of rest, an iteration of the Bible's "And the Lord rested on that day." It was a Jewish gift to the world, she thought with pride. She took a seat in an empty row at the back so she could be alone with her thoughts.

Lila loved particularly the Sabbath selection that the congregation often read. It was written by Rabbi Abraham Joshua Heschel, and tonight the congregation was reciting it in unison.

> There is a song in the wind and joy in the trees,
> The Sabbath arrives in the world, scattering
> a song in the silence of the night.
> Eternity ushers a day.

Her feeling of peacefulness enveloped her only to be abruptly overturned.

The temple bulletin listed the anniversary of members' deaths so relatives could say the *Yahrzeit* prayer in their memory. As she scanned the pages, she felt the blood rush to her face when she saw on the list the name Leo Shechter, Mort and Marla's father. She took a deep breath. Calm down, she told herself. Mort would commemorate his father in the Reform shul.

She began to follow the prayers, trying to concentrate, reading the Hebrew and checking with the English to see the meanings. She sensed someone had taken the seat next to hers, but she didn't look around; she closed her eyes to regain her sense of peace while the cantor sang.

When they were asked to stand for the opening of the ark, she placed her prayer book in the rack and rose, her hand on the top of the wooden seat in front of her. A man's hand touched hers. She looked down. She saw the fine blond hairs on his fingers. Her heart was pounding. The congregation sang on. The organ music reached a crescendo. The man's warm hand covered hers. Her mouth fell open in wonder. Slowly she turned her hand around to grasp his.

They stood there silently, not looking at one another, reciting together the prayer in the memory of his father and the others who were being remembered, until the rabbi added a blessing ending in a triumphant "Shabbat shalom!" Then the silent couple turned to face each other, their eyes brimming.

"Do I have you back?" Mort whispered.

"I'm here for you forever, if you wish it," Lila said, a smile breaking through her troubled gaze.

"Forever," Mort said. Then they embraced, and their lips met in what was no ordinary Shabbat shalom.

"How did you know to come tonight?" Lila asked in a happy daze.

"I didn't know you'd be here. I was sitting on the side when I saw you. I couldn't believe it. Scott just called this afternoon to tell me his aunt said your divorce was final. I was so happy I just wanted to be here to give thanks and remember my dad. I was going to call tonight, no matter the time. And here we are!"

"Dr. Mort," shouted Chloe, released from the junior services. She ran to hug him.

He scooped her up in a bear hug. Then set her down.

"Chloe, you wunderkind. Let me see how you've grown!"

"Where is Andrea?" Chloe demanded.

"Come, we'll pick her up. She's at a friend's house."

"We are all together again," the girl declared with finality, to no one in particular.

———

They were married in Rabbi Newman's chapel with Rabbi Gordon in attendance.

The children's aunts and uncles, the Goldrings, and friends from both synagogues were in the pews and even Alan Freed, chairman of the board of Temple Beth El came to wish them well. There was a catered dinner in the Shechter Social Hall and a string quartet that played the music for an endless hora, the gathering danced with their children.

Once school was out that summer, the Shechter foursome traveled to Israel to see the sights and watch some of the matches taking place during the Maccabiah games. They saw the windsurfers on the Mediterranean from the beach in Tel Aviv and cheered for an American boy from New York even though he did not win. They wandered the stony paths of the Old City in Jerusalem. They learned the history of Yemin Moshe, the windmill in a park near the King David Hotel.

When they returned to their hotel, Mort's "girls" went upstairs to freshen up and change for dinner. He visited the jeweler in the hotel and then took the elevator to their floor. He knocked at the door. "Come in," came a chorus.

He grinned at his trio and gave Lila a long blue jeweler's box. Inside she found a string of pearls and earrings to match. Lila eyes widened at the gift. She removed her *hamsa* from around her neck to allow Mort to put on the warmly glowing strand. "They're beautiful," she said softly. "You shouldn't have. This trip was special enough. But thank you, Mort, thank you. I love them." She touched her lips to the amulet in her hand before stowing it in her purse. This little *hamsa* brought me the best of luck, after all, she thought to herself. And I have a surprise for Mort later. She smiled happily. We're to have a baby.

Chapter 32

In the spring of 2009, Lila Shechter sat in the living room of her comfortable home reading a letter. It was from Betty Lou Brown.

It said that Mollie was fifteen and would be a senior in high school the following year. Betty Lou wrote that she had received a letter from a lawyer stating that a sum of money had been deposited by him in the bank to be delivered to Mollie Brown and Chloe Ostro when they were ready for college. He was prepared to make the distribution. The donor, who had made arrangements with him thirteen years earlier, was Alton Ostro.

Lila felt dizzy. She had forgotten that whole painful relationship in her happiness with Mort, Andrea, Chloe, and Lee, their twelve-year-old son. Now the ogre was on the scene again to confuse and distress her. All the time, he did have some feeling for his girls. He claimed he was indigent because his monies were put aside safely for the girls. Her mother's words came back to her—"There is goodness in all people." Yes, Mama, how sad. What a complex, disturbing man. He will be my lifelong regret.

Many years earlier, when Chloe was ten, she had told her about her half-sister. Chloe was excited; she wanted to meet her. Lila suggested they become pen pals. Secretly, the girls did more than that, e-mailing each other about their lives and hoping, some day, to meet. Chloe begged her mother to take her to Perryville to Mollie to see her father's barn and one of his chairs. When Chloe was twelve, Lila finally agreed. They flew to Asheville. Betty Lou picked them up at the airport. The two girls sat in the back of the van, looking at each other, shy at first, but then talking about school and subjects they liked.

When they arrived in Perryville, Lila wanted to show Chloe where her father lived. The barn was no longer there. A developer had bought the land and had put up a tract of homes on the site.

Betty Lou visited Alton every few months. His prison was in the eastern part of the state, a four-hour ride from Perryville. She said he was in a lot of pain. "He has arthritis, his hands are gnarled and always hurt, yet he still works in the prison carpentry shop—yes, fixing chairs."

Years ago, when Raymond brought him papers to sign relinquishing his parental rights to Chloe so Mort could adopt her, he gave Alton a top-of-the-line radio with earphones to enable him to enjoy music in his off hours. Earlier, he had met him when he signed the divorce papers. Alton was silent during these visits, nodding and signing with his right hand.

"I bring him the plum cake he likes," Betty Lou said while they were having lunch in the Perryville cafe. "He also asked for hard cheddar."

"We want to see our father," Mollie said.

"I do too, Mom," Chloe added. Both women frowned.

"When you are older, not before," Betty Lou said with authority.

"You can write to him, if you like," Lila ventured. "If that's okay with you, Betty Lou?"

"I think that's a nice idea. Send him drawings you've done. But, haha, don't expect an answer."

Mollie had come to visit the Shechters when she was older.

"Cora," Lila said, "I'm catching up to you. We have his, mine, and ours in one household plus a visiting half-sister."

The two girls were compatible, both interested in science. A trip was made to the University of Pittsburgh and to Carnegie-Mellon to scope them out. These institutions were renowned for research and top-ranked departments of science. Chloe was interested in environmental science; Mollie in computers.

When the grant came in from Ostro's lawyer, both girls insisted that it was time they visited their "sperm donor," as Mollie called him. She knew that Ostro had paid her little attention, but she was four when he was incarcerated, and she remembered him. Chloe had no recollection of her father. She loved Mort and called him Dad without reservation, but she was curious. The sisters also wanted to thank Ostro in person. They had written to him over the years, receiving no response, but they understood he was the silent man. Mort offered to accompany Chloe to the prison, but she felt she could handle it herself. After her flight to Asheville, she shared the driving with Betty Lou.

The reality of the prison shook both girls. "This is awful," Mollie said as they went through several menacing-looking gates.

The visitors' room was bare except for the partitioned interviewing table that stretched the length of the room.

Alton was brought in wearing his tan prison garb. Betty Lou spoke to him first. "Alton, dear. Your daughters are here to say hello to you. Remember Chloe and Mollie. They are friends now."

At the mention of Chloe, Betty Lou thought she saw Alton wince. She stepped back. The girls approached him, two fresh-faced teenagers in the bloom of youth, Mollie more buxom than Chloe who was slim with an athletic bearing.

Alton said nothing. He looked up and then down. The girls too were tongue-tied, scanning the features of the gray-haired man with deep lines etched in his face and dark rings under his eyes.

"Are you feeling all right, Daddy?" asked Mollie.

He looked at the speaker without recognition.

Chloe thought she would begin to cry. She gave up her seat to Betty Lou. Mollie and her mother spoke to Alton for a while, then she motioned to the guard to take the cake she had brought. Alton looked at her, as if to say, "Enough."

"Alton, say good-bye to Mollie and Chloe, and don't forget to ask for your plum cake."

"Thank you, Betty Lou," he whispered hoarsely. "Thank you for bringing the cheerleaders." Chloe managed a smile to him as he rose to go. Betty Lou put her arm around Chloe. "This was so hard for you, honey."

"It's totally horrible," Chloe said. "It's so terrible to know your father is a criminal. He looks like he should be in a hospital with someone to care for him. I can't imagine my mother with him. And he's such a physical and mental wreck. How long does he have to be here?"

"It's hard to know, three more years possibly."

"If he is let out, how will he manage? He gave us his money. I'll be working to pay him back," Chloe said with resolve.

"Me too, we'll take care of him," Mollie added.

"That's very nice, girls, but not very possible. I'll keep him posted on your progress in college. He may say nothing, but I think he cares. Now cheer up, you're cheerleaders, remember." They gave her grim smiles.

Chloe spoke to her parents about the visit. "The important thing to me is what will he do when he is released, which may be in three years?"

"We'll see that he has an appropriate living arrangement then," Mort said.

"The man is so broken. It's so sad," she added wistfully.

"Chloe, I've spoken with Betty Lou, she wants to look after him. By then she will retire. Her legs are giving out— all that standing for years on end. We of course will help her if that's what she wants, and we both agreed to go before the parole board on his behalf. You're not to worry,"

"I want to be involved somehow," Chloe stated. "It's pretty confusing, knowing he is my father, that he was once so well respected, and now—it's awful." Chloe looked at her parents for an answer.

Lila shook her head. "I don't know what more I could have done. But it will always be my question, and it will always haunt me that I hid our survival," she said sadly. She glanced at Mort.

"You are proof, Chloe, that the man has people who care about his welfare," he said. "He is not alone anymore." He sighed and was silent.

Chloe picked up that the subject was a painful one for her parents. She smiled at them. Maybe someday she would have to be the wise one. Best leave it for now. "Promise to keep me posted," she said. "Okay?"

Mort and Lila agreed, with warm feelings for the distressed child.

By the time Ostro's grant had been received Chloe was a sophomore at Pitt. Mollie immediately said she wanted to go there. Chloe had a small state scholarship, and Mollie hoped for a larger one. As an out-of-state student, costs would put attending the college out of range for Betty Lou, even with Ostro's help. The following year, she was admitted with a substantial grant-in-aid. She came to the Shechters for the send-off.

There was a big party that flowed from the living room and den onto the lawn. Martin, Cora, Sara, and Brett and his wife, Mahalia, whom he had met when he was an exchange student in Russia, were there, plus a host of temple friends. Judith had flown in to stay with them. Harvey couldn't get away. Andrew Wong brought his mom. Andrew was a senior at Carnegie-Melon. Andrea, who had grown into a tall friendly young woman, looking not unlike her mother Susan's portrait, introduced her current boyfriend, a law student at Penn. There was a lot of college rivalry among the young people, each one standing up for his or her own school, until the party broke up and the college crowd left to go to a local hangout. With the other adults gone, Judith and Amy Wong, who was waiting for Andrew's return, sat in the living room talking about their lives. Lee ran upstairs to his video games.

Mort and Lila were teary-eyed as they cleaned up in the kitchen. "We did good," Mort said. "I think our kids are terrific."

"Mort, dearest, I'm so glad Lee is still young enough to be home. I don't know how I'll handle it when he goes off."

"I wouldn't worry too much. By then you'll be a grandma," Mort teased. Lila dried her hands and brought Mort's face toward hers.

The next morning, Mort and Lila were to drive the girls to college. As they left the house amid kisses and hugs from Judith and Lee, he called out to Mollie, "Don't forget to come back in May for my bar mitzvah!"

CPSIA information can be obtained at www.ICGtesting.com
Printed in the USA
LVOW07s0329251014

410431LV00001B/33/P